Battleworld

BATTLEWORLD

Martin K. Kelemen

iUniverse LLC
Bloomington

BATTLEWORLD

This is a work of fiction. All of the characters, names, incidents, organizations, and dialogue in this novel are either the products of the author's imagination or are used fictitiously.

iUniverse books may be ordered through booksellers or by contacting:

iUniverse LLC
1663 Liberty Drive
Bloomington, IN 47403
www.iuniverse.com
1-800-Authors (1-800-288-4677)

Because of the dynamic nature of the Internet, any web addresses or links contained in this book may have changed since publication and may no longer be valid. The views expressed in this work are solely those of the author and do not necessarily reflect the views of the publisher, and the publisher hereby disclaims any responsibility for them.

Any people depicted in stock imagery provided by Thinkstock are models, and such images are being used for illustrative purposes only. Certain stock imagery © Thinkstock.

ISBN: 978-1-4917-2015-8 (sc)
ISBN: 978-1-4917-2016-5 (e)

Printed in the United States of America.

iUniverse rev. date: 02/06/2014

To my first love, my best friend, and everyone out there living in their own world.

Dedicated to Elaine

GRATITUDE

I thank my open-minded sister and aunt, for correcting my mistakes.

I thank my elementary/middle school, which inspired me to write this.

I thank my family, for being supportive.

And I thank everyone who took interest in Battleworld, ever since I told them I was writing it.

PROLOGUE

Once upon a time, in a far off world, people were born with special powers. Over time, as these warriors grew, they decided to make various schools in which they would teach the new generation how to use their powers properly. This is a story of a young warrior, one who wishes to rid the world of all that is evil, and of his journey . . .

CHAPTER 1

INTRODUCTION

"Are you getting ready for tomorrow?" Barney asked instantly.

"Um . . . yeah, sure . . ." Elaine answered very shyly.

She was like that. Elaine. Very shy, yet she always felt the need to say what she thought out loud. And it's not like she hadn't acted on it, but around people she didn't know, she never mouthed out a single word. Barney, on the other hand, was a hot-headed "cool" guy, very easy to like. I was a bit of both.

Barney was fat. He did have muscle, but he was chubby. I wouldn't exactly describe him as "build up". He also had really long light brown hair, but it wasn't long like in a girl, it was more like that of a lion. Elaine had average length dark brown hair, and topaz orange eyes. Her eyes really are the most beautiful ones I had ever seen. And she had a great body, but more on that later.

"How about you, Martin?" he asked.

"I don't have to be excited, I know I'm going to win." I replied without any interest. The truth is, I was very excited about the tournament, as always, but I didn't want Barney to know because then he would talk about it until the very second the tournament started.

"Of course you aren't." Barney said with a fair doze of sarcasm.

Unlike Barney, I was very hard to like. I'm full of myself, cruel yet kind, and very attractive, if I may add. My name is Martin Killman Kelemen. Most people call me Kelemen, or Killman, or really anything they make out of it, but close friends call me Martin. I'm a dark brown haired guy, not popular with girls (although they love me, they just don't wanna admit it), and I really do have a great body.

Then, out of nowhere, popped out our class-mistress. She was a wise, blond haired woman with mysterious brown eyes. Each class has one. We are the 7th graders, 7. C. Greatest in our generation. By grades, anyway.

"Heading off home, eh?" she asked.

"Yes, well, we were training and it got late, and we have to go to sleep early, to be ready for the tournament." Elaine answered with her sweet voice.

"All right then. I won't keep you. Good luck tomorrow. Make me proud, as always."

"Thank you, class-mistress!" all three of us responded at the same time. We then sat down on a bench, just outside of the school, and started talking.

"At the last year interschool tournament, the winner was Grimley Binemme. He could call various animals, which then helped him later in combat." Barney said, as if he was speaking of a legend. Well, Grimley was kind of a legend among our circles. He treats animals as his family, and can call them into battle at any time he pleases, all features of the Binemme clan; and that is probably why he won, his teamwork really is flawless. Though I doubt he could go toe to toe with me.

"Ugh! You just don't get it! It doesn't matter who won last year, it matters who'll win now." Elaine said very angrily. As for our abilities, Barney was big and he had strong punches, while Elaine was average height, great ass (you know you're thinking it), and was from the Enrik clan. Now the Enrik clan members could easily locate one's energy, and used their own "Enrik energy" to hit enemies. This came quite in handy, especially since said energy is invisible. The Enrik could also see the body of any being with their nerve system, and the precise location of the heart.

And me? I'm super fast, and also I like using lightning, because I can combine it with my speed. Since I'm from the Kelemen clan, I'll soon get (I at least hope) the Kelemen swords, the unbreakable swords in which an owner of the sword can seal any person he stabbed with it in another dimension inside the sword, as long as the sword remains in the body of the victim until they are sealed. Like I said, I haven't acquired the Kelemen swords yet. It is said that they present themselves to a Kelemen clan member when they deserve them. And, only a Kelemen can wield the swords. Also, the Kelemen who sealed the person can use their power. For an example, if I were to seal Elaine, I could use the Enrik clan attacks.

But more important than that, lately, I started thinking Barney had a crush on Elaine. He looks at her differently, ever since she saved his life. At the beginning of the year, our school was attacked by Swaltagar, a spider like human being who possesses the power of making spider web, is also very fast and punches really hard, with his four arms. I heard from a teacher he was a failed biological experiment, but there's no proof of that. The teachers (also known as the techs) managed to beat him, though he swore revenge on our school. Barney got caught in the middle, and Elaine saved him in the nick of time.

Anyway, he looks at her as he looks at a giant chicken after training for three days non-stop.

Now don't get me wrong, this isn't some kind of a love triangle. I think of Elaine as my archrival, not as my girlfriend. Although Barney is my best friend, I treat him as a rival as well.

"So, Elaine, um . . . would you care to go out with me some time?" Barney asked, very nervously.

"Yeah, we should all go to Elydorf's!" she answered with great enthusiasm. You see, Elaine loved Elydorf's because they served her favorite drink, pear cocktail, while Barney and I hated that place because they didn't serve our favorite drink, anything with no pear in it. Elydorf's was named after Elydorf, the wizard who saved the world from certain defeat many years ago.

"Badger's Honor! No freaking way! I'm not going there!"

"Me neither" I said angrily.

"You guys are such buzzkills" Elaine said, very annoyed.

"About the tournament," I said "if I get chosen to fight one of you, I won't hold back, and I expect you to do the same."

"Please Martin, who do you take us for? Of course we're gonna bring it, and we're gonna bring it hard!" Elaine proclaimed, full of thrill. We talked a little while longer, left our school, the school of St. Atlas, said our good lucks and goodbyes and went to our homes.

Looking back, things were so simple then . . .

CHAPTER 2

7TH GRADERS INTERSCHOOL TOURNAMENT

So the day finally came. The Interschool Tournament. Every year, the 7th graders are tested, and the winner's school is declared the best. Since our school is the oldest, we are hosting it. The tournament means so much to St. Atlas that we can't lose. It's basically tradition for us to win. As I was leaving home, I packed my calling ball (each warrior is given one at birth, for calling various things/creatures into battle). It works simple, really. You just have to squeeze the ball, and the thing you wish to call into battle shall appear, provided that you have both enough energy to call the thing you wish to call and it in your calling storage, an infinite, empty dimension in which every warrior's callings are saved. I then rushed to the school to see the contestants.

And the school was at its peak. The giant brown walls that represented the darkness and harshness of the tournament, the watching arena, rising from the fighting arena, stood there not for parents, but for warriors participating in the tournament and the teachers. I looked around, seeing if anybody familiar from other schools was here.

That's when I heard the announcement.

"Welcome to the 14th annual 7th graders Interschool Tournament! Today the 7th graders from the School of St. Atlas are competing with various students from other schools for the school's title of the best! The tournament will begin in one hour, and now a message from St. Atlas's headmaster." The long dark brown haired 40 or so year old woman spoke.

"Warriors, contestants from all schools, I personally welcome you to this tournament. Fight, for your school, for your family's honor, and for the right to be the best."

"Wow," I thought—"the competition here is unbelievable."

I checked who is it that I'm fighting in the first match on the board. I couldn't believe my eyes. My first opponent was Anne Kitty from class 7. A. She is beautiful to some people yet to others (me) she was ugly. Her nose is unusually large. She isn't the strongest warrior, but she uses her voice as a weapon. I have to watch out for that. Barney is going to fight Neven Sonny, a guy from our class with the ability of turning into a giant ball, while Elaine was chosen to fight John II. in the first round. John is also in our class, he uses lightning and is pretty muscular, though a bit stunted. He has short blonde hair and emerald eyes, but he is irritating, thus not popular with girls. I was going to check the other match ups, but I went to my favorite place instead, the stairs behind the magic closet. I like that place, it's very quiet, even on such a day. I heard a noise in the hallway, so I hid and listened.

"Are you crazy? We have to win for our school! Tech Nimmie was very specific. Win the tournament. If one of us doesn't, our school won't be the best, and we will be treated like jokes again!" the mysterious girl said. She had dark, black hair, and a necklace with an illustration of a lamb.

"Relax, sis, I'm pretty sure one of us will win." the boy she was talking to replied. Unlike the girl, the boy had white hair, and looked like a typical teenager. Well, except for the white hair, obviously.

"We'd better, or it's back to being losers for us." she said, after which stormed off quickly. Her brother followed suit.

"What was that?" I thought as I returned to the arena. Before I knew it, the first match had started.

That girl I heard talking earlier was fighting in the first round. Her opponent was a tough looking guy; looked like he was from another era, he had short brown hair, and brown eyes.

"Match No. 1! Letizia Trotten vs. Ivory Bianco—Begin."

The big guy, Ivory, started.

"I eat girls like you for breakfast!" he said as he marched at her. He tried to punch her, but as his hand was closing in on her face, a huge barrier of lava protected her.

"Ugh!" Ivory screamed in pain.

"That's funny" Lettie said—"I didn't think you possessed the ability to eat. Now to finish this Lava Garden: Attack Of Dolomite!"

As those words were spoken, a huge pile of lava from the ground flew up and landed on Ivory's body.

He disappeared from the Mighty Shield, and returned to the watching arena.

The Mighty Shield is any space protected by 4 blue-like walls. Nothing gets in, nothing gets out, until one is defeated, surrenders, or is unable to continue the fight.

And when the loser returns to the watching arena (thus exiting/disappearing from the Mighty Shield), all his/her wounds are restored to his state before he/she entered the arena. This is only used in schools in school tournaments and matches. It prevents students from dying for the sake of the tournament. But there was a time when it didn't exist. A dark time soaked with more blood than anyone can imagine.

Next match is Barney's.

"Round 2: Barney" the crowd started cheering—"vs. Neven Sonny—Begin!"

Barney attacked first, and as he rushed to him, Neven turned into a ball and countered Barney's rush.

Barney's fist and Neven (as a ball) clashed. Neven repelled Barney, and knocked him to a wall. He then returned to his normal form, jumped in the air, and landed on Barney. He punctured his lungs and broke his collarbone. Barney couldn't breathe. He returned to the watching arena after he lost in the Mighty Shield.

"The winner is Neven Sonny!" the announcer said, full of enthusiasm.

The crowd couldn't believe their eyes. Neven Sonny, getting a drop on Barney Buttons.

"Quite impressive, yet so dumb. The one that the crowd loves lost, and the obvious loser won."

"Matej?" I asked, surprised. I then turned around and saw him. It really was Matej Bridgeman, my Anena. In OSW, Organization of Speed Warriors (a group of people learning advanced speed techniques) that we both attend, you need to have a partner, someone who will work with you and save you, if you were to find yourself in danger. These are called Anenas. He's my Anena, and I'm his. Anenas can also combine to create an even mightier warrior. Matej attends the school of St. Andrew; he is an 8th grader.

"I just couldn't miss watching you get your ass kicked, Martin," he said with a smile on his face.

"Are you up next?"

"Yes."

"In that case, break a leg. See you after you lose." he said.

Matej Bridgeman was a lot like me. Almost everyone in OSW is like me. He was a tall guy, dark brown hair and forest green eyes. He always wore a t-shirt with the Bridgeman clan symbol on it, every day a differently colored one, of course. The symbol was a lion in an armor. It represented the "strongest warrior", the one who will lead others. Ah. Bridgemen and their obsession with being the strongest. He is, needless to say, of the Bridgeman clan. The Bridgeman clan could slow time, and Matej likes combining that with his speed. He also uses water attacks a lot.

CHAPTER 3

MY MATCH

So it finally came. My match. I know I'm going to fight Anne, but I still feel nervous. Guess it's just normal to feel like that. I changed my clothes, from a plain bright orange t-shirt and sapphire blue jeans to my uniform, a black diver-like suit. I usually don't fight in this "uniform", but I'll make an exception for the tournament. It's on.

"Round 3: Anne Kitty vs. Martin Kelemen—Begin."

Anne touched her vocal folds, and focused her energy there. I rushed to hit her, but as I closed in, she started to sing. Her voice was so hypnotizing, I could barely move. I fell on the floor, and she took out her medium length knife and tried to cut my throat. I quickly grabbed her leg and sent her mind in a world of illusions. She managed to break out of my mind game, dropped the knife, and we both backed away from each other and returned to our original positions. I know she is going to hypnotize me again, and I still haven't fully recovered from the first time she sang. She was starting to sing again; that's when I realized what I had to do. I pretended to subdue to her hypnotization and fell on the floor. This made her stop singing. I continued pretending I was helpless. She rushed at me with her fist, I took that knife she dropped earlier and as she was trying to punch me, I cut her vocal folds.

She couldn't scream. I quickly charged my arm with lightning, and pierced her body three times: the kidney, the lungs and the heart. Again, she teleported to the watching arena, and remained unharmed. I am so grateful we have this system; I don't have to hold back.

"The winner is Martin Kelemen."

Three hours later and all the other matches were finished. Elaine managed to beat John, and she mocked Barney for having lost the match. The announcer then announced the next fight.

"Round 1, 2nd period:

Matthew Alajko vs. Letizia Trotten—Begin."

So much for the heads up.

"I'll win, just surrender, or I'll make it painful for you" she said.

"Calling: Giant's bat!" Matthew said, ignoring all of Lettie's words.

"Getting straight to the point, eh? In that case, I'll get serious too. Lava Crowd: Lava Waterfall!"

A giant mass of lava that suddenly appeared out of the walls attacked Matthew from all sides, but he repelled it with his bat, and then attacked Lettie with it; though her shield of lava protected her.

"You're good . . . but unfortunately for you it takes more than "just good" to beat Letizia Trotten."

Matthew's bat melted, so he charged at her. Lettie easily burned his feet, and then covered his whole body in lava. Matthew had lost. But before it was officially declared, his body exploded. It seems he placed mini bombs around him, probably used to monitor his heartbeat so that if his heart would stop beating, Lettie would lose as well, and therefore no contestant would pass. Clever. Unfortunately, the lava shield kicked in just in time and saved her.

"The winner is Lettie." the announcer announced, now calling Letizia by her nickname.

"Quite impressive, the Goth girl, I mean." Matej said, appearing out of nowhere.

"Round 2, 2nd period:
Richard Trotten vs. Michael Motto"

Michael, like Matthew, goes to our class. He is from the Motto clan, meaning his body can adapt to that of any animal he imagines. Also, Richard must be related to Lettie, considering they have the same last name.

"Begin."

For this match, Michael chose the leopard. He quickly jumped towards Richard, but he suddenly began moving really slowly. It seems Richard slowed time. He then summoned up all his energy, fired a blast from his arm, and blasted the leopard-adapted Michael away. The blast blew him to pieces. Michael then teleported to the watching arena.

"The winner is Richard Trotten."

"Richard Trotten, eh? If he can stop time, he must be of my clan. But I'm afraid that's not the case." Matej said, very concerned.

"Why?" I simply asked.

"Because" he continued to talk "look at his hands. There is no Bridgering on his left index. And every Bridgeman has one."

"Ok, so basically what you're saying is that this guy isn't a Bridgeman because there's no little ring on his finger?" I said.

"It's a clan tradition. Even our rogues respect it, to my displeasure. In any event, our theories don't matter" Matej said, looking at me "what matters is that he is probably some kind of a failed biological experiment, or even worse. His full abilities are yet unknown to us, and we fear what we don't know."

"Round 3, 2nd period:
Neven Sonny vs. Martin Kelemen—Begin!"

Whoa, I'm already up again. Well, I might as well get this over with, and then rub it in Barney's face.

Neven turned into a ball and attacked me. How original. I threw a lightning bomb at him, and after it hit, it exploded, as expected. He remained unharmed, so I repeated the process ten more times. It didn't help. He hit me and knocked me into a wall. Ouch. He then jumped and tried to do the same thing to me as he did to Barney, although this time he was in his ball state, but I managed to dodge. Then I trapped him with earth pillars, which he easily broke out of, and tried to attack me, however, just before he hit me, he returned to his human form, injured.

Those lightning bombs did hurt him! He wasn't able to move. Needless to say, I won.

"The winner is Martin K. Kelemen."

"The fat boy fell, I felt that." Matej said immediately after I won the match. The next one was with that guy Lettie was talking to, her brother.

Next was Domenic vs. Zannibi.

Domenic went to our class, similar looks to mine, but everyone seemed to like him more than they liked me, which I can't possibly see why. I'm not jealous or anything, but still.

He quickly attacked Zannibi, throwing a ball of energy at him. It did little damage so he kicked the ball, and it hit him in the face. Since that also didn't work, he did it again. And again. Seriously, after a while it seemed that Domenic had nothing better to do than shoot fast balls in Zannibi's face.

"If you're done, I would like to kill you now." Zannibi said. Domenic hit him again.

"I'll take that as a yes. Calling: 2 x Zombie!"

As Zannibi said that, two zombies emerged out of the ground and attacked Domenic. He tried to repel them with everything he had, but he couldn't, and so they beat him. Well, tore him apart is more likely, but still.

"The winner is Zannibi Trotten."

CHAPTER 4

QUARTER AND SEMI-FINALS

"The match ups for the quarter finals that will take place in half an hour are as follows:"

The announcer announced the match ups, but all I got was that I'm fighting Lettie, and that both her brothers and Elaine are in the quarter finals as well.

"Looks like you got the lava girl." Matej said.

"Best of luck!"

"Thanks." I replied happily.

Half an hour passed like a minute does.

Elaine won her match, and now it's my turn.

"Round 2 of the quarter finals:
Martin Kelemen vs. Letizia Trotten—Begin."

"You will lose for sure, pretty boy" she blew me a kiss.

"I'll probably enjoy this more than I should" I said loudly, untouched by her "kiss".

I started off with a lightning bomb. I can use this attack due to my Stodyanna genes, just like all my lightning-based attacks.

Her lava blocked the hit. As expected.

"Lava Prison: Full Onslaught!"

4 pillars of lava emerged and from the top of each pillar a string of lava attacked me.

"Calling: Neron!"

Neron is my pet scorpion. I like scorpions. He is a coal-black 6 feet tall giant forest scorpion and can block almost any attack with his organic armor. I quickly hid in him (he opened the armor, closed it when I got in), before Lettie's lava got to me, and remained unharmed. Neron then disappeared (I reverse-called him), after which I ran and got behind Lettie. I enhanced my arm with lightning, and tried to hit her, but she blocked my arm with lava, without even turning her head.

"Ugh" I screamed.

"Now to finish you off: Lava World." she said.

The arena filled up with lava, up to 6 feet tall. Lettie grew wings made of lava and flew up. I jumped and used the earth from the wall right to me as a platform, manipulating the earth so that I could attach it to my feet. I knew there had to be something I could do. And that's when I saw it. Her wings were made out of fire, not lava. They were fire red, not lava red. The distinction between the two shades of red catches my eye because my mother is an artist.

I fired a narrow, bridge-like lightning blast at her but she shielded herself with her wings. I jumped and launched my water vomit; a blast of water emerged from my mouth and targeted her wings. It hit, drying the wings, and soon both Lettie and I were falling into what was now a little over than 8 feet of lava. She started removing the lava from her side of the arena, so I threw a lightning bomb at her. For the lava to protect her, she had to remove the lava from the floor, which resulted in her falling there, and in her breaking her spine. However, the lightning bomb managed to hit her, so she fell to her doom faster than I did. The moment she broke her spine, both she and I got out of the Mighty Shield.

"The winner is Martin Kelemen."

The Trotten brothers also won their matches.

Time for the semifinals.

I was chosen to fight Zannibi Trotten, while Elaine got his brother Richard.

First up is Elaine's fight.

"Round 1 of the semifinals: Begin."

"Enrik: Heart Stop" Elaine controlled her Enrik energy to stop Richard's heart.

Richard's heart, however, did not stop.

"Enrik: Nerve Destruction!"

Still nothing. I am afraid of this guy. First he uses Bridgeman attacks, then he takes no damage from Enrik attacks . . . who is he?

"Ok, now you're starting to irritate me. Enrik:" "Bridgeman: Imperial Time Stop x 10!" he interrupted her. Time slowed down and he blasted her, firing a giant blast of energy from his right arm. Elaine survived because of her Enrik shield. But she couldn't survive the next blast, which was at full power.

"The winner is Richard Trotten!"

"I don't believe this. He can clearly use Bridgeman attacks . . . I must report this to dad and the others. I shall go now. See ya." Matej ran away.

"Zannibi Trotten vs. Martin Kelemen—Begin!"

It's quite silly how quickly a match can start.

"Calling: 2 x zombie." he said.

I threw two lightning bombs at the zombies and they exploded.

"Is that all you got?" I asked.

"Let's see if you'll survive this. Calling: 100 x Zombie!" he shouted.

One hundred zombies emerged out of the ground. Great. I'm screwed. It doesn't matter; I'll shoot them all. I tried to do that, but they were too fast, too swift. Finally I enhanced my arms with lightning, went on a freakin' rampage, and killed all one hundred of them.

"That's good, but you still lose. Calling: 100 x Zombie!" as he spoke those words, I fired a water vomit at him. He dodged, but the water remained, behind him. Before I knew it, a hundred more zombies attacked me. I killed about twenty-four with my bare arms, but then they captured me. They tried to decapitate me, but I quickly teleported out of that mass of water, behind Zannibi. I enhanced my right arm with lightning yet again, and almost stabbed him, but a zombie sacrificed himself in his place. I returned to my original position, killing the rest of the zombies while doing so. I firmly gripped my veins, water teleportation would make anyone sick, let alone a non-water user. Then Zannibi said: "Okay, round 3: Calling: 100 x Zombie!"

Nothing happened.

"I said: Calling: 100 x Zombie!" he repeated, furiously, like a spoiled brat.

Still, nothing happened.

"Do you realize now that you're no match for me" I continued "because you cannot call anymore. I burned your fingertips. You can no longer call."

The fingertips are the second requirement for calling things into battle, next to the calling ball. And I managed to burn his with my lightning when I teleported out of the water vomit.

I quickly ran behind him.

"Game over."

As I was trying to run my lightning enhanced arm through his heart, a giant zombie emerged out of the ground.

"This is my zombie guard" Zannibi chuckled.

What, did he sign a contract with the zombies? Perfect. Just freaking perfect. Only one way out of this.

"Stodyanna: Plasma Bolt!" I said, charging my arm with lightning. It was too much though, my body weakened and was electrocuted. I attacked the big zombie, running up to him and piercing his left leg with my ultra-charged lightning arm. He took no damage. But then, 5 seconds later, lightning electrocuted him. The same lightning I infected him with 5 second ago. I also attacked Zannibi with the same attack, but he dodged my arm. However, a few seconds later, lightning electrocuted him as well, because it managed to enter his body.

"The winner is"

Ouch. I felt something. A big, ugly hand ran through my heart.

"This is me at my full power." Zannibi said, completely transformed into a zombie.

His skin hardened, it became grey. His face looked like it was from the scariest horror movie ever. He threw me against a wall. Luckily, I managed to turn into a vampire just before he pierced my heart. Yes, I'm from the Ryunichi clan, the vampire clan. In most cases, I wouldn't make the transformation in time, but I expected Zannibi to turn into a zombie. He's the type of guy that'd do anything to win; even if it means zombifying himself.

"Quite impressive, but now we shall see who's the stronger monster." I said, full of bloodlust. I rushed to him and bit him on the neck. I'm much faster now that I'm a vampire, but he's even faster in his zombified state. He repelled me, and once again threw me against the wall.

"Ryunichi: Blood Explosion!" I said, with my lips drenched in blue, zombie blood.

Zannibi exploded, and his blood was all over the place. I thought I had won, but he quickly appeared behind me.

"Zombie Attack of All Generations!" he shouted. Before I knew it, countless zombies were attacking me from every angle. I had to escape.

"Didn't think you could fool me twice, now did you? Substituting another zombie was easy once I caught onto your pattern of attack. You sting, then you wait, and bam-you win, as easy as that." Zannibi bragged.

The zombies then disappeared.

"I win" Zannibi stated.

"Oh." I started "I beg to differ."

"How d-did y-you survive?" he stuttered.

"Didn't you know," I said "that vampires turn into bats?"

I revealed myself to him. I transformed myself completely into a bat, though I was still shaped like a human. Dark-brown wings, wide eyes, medium-size fangs, and hair all over my body.

I grabbed Zannibi and flew up in the air, with my bat-shaped wings. I then dropped him, head first. I thought I had won, but he managed to turn into an even uglier zombie. Just how much stages of transformation does this guy have?

"I've inserted my predecessor's DNA into my body, so that it makes me stronger. And now you die." he said. I know I have to use black magic, also known as Damaken. But Damaken is pretty hard to control. To begin with, it's black magic. Your soul becomes pretty dark once you use it. You enter a certain state, and it reflects on your physical and mental abilities. But I had no choice.

"Damaken: Release!" I said loudly. My appearance was also different. I returned to my normal form, and my eyes were much darker. As Zannibi rushed at me, I said "Damaken: Saints' Statues!"

Then, out of the walls, appeared statues with images of various saints. Zannibi was paralyzed and I took his soul out with my Damaken: Sacred Steal.

"You are the one who's dying." I said, as his soul was poured out of his body. Of course, he won't actually die; he'll just be teleported back to the watching arena, but still. The longest battle I've ever been in.

"Finally, the winner is Martin Kelemen," said the announcer, with a sigh of relief, since our match was finally over. And so were the semifinals.

CHAPTER 5

INVESTIGATIONS

"You can now all return to class. The finals will take place tomorrow." the headmaster gave an announcement. All of us were confused. We thought they would take place now. And so, we went to class. Everyone who wasn't from our school went back to their homes, though they would come tomorrow, to watch the finals, of course.

As I went to class, a surprise was waiting for me.

"All praise our hero!" everyone shouted.

My class. Matthew, John II., Max, Victoria, Domenic, Neven, Jaden J, Michael, Elaine, Tom, Horvath, Heather, Proshko, Macy, Benji, Barney and Johnny. And of course, our class-mistress.

"You beat me fair and square, Martin. Now everyone knows the secret to beating me. Means I'll just have to up my game a bit." Neven said, shaking my hand.

I smiled. He is one of my better friends.

"It is said that the 6th graders will watch the fight tomorrow, too. That means everyone will. We are counting on you." said Horvath.

Right. No pressure there.

"Why don't you just stop bothering our hero? Of course he'll win!" said Jaden J, very enthusiastically.

"But" Elaine added "that Richard guy is really weird. He took no damage from my attacks at all. And he can slow time. You have to beat him, for our school, and to avenge mine and Michael's defeat."

"She's right about that." Michael said.

The class soon ended. I went home. I tried to understand this Richard character. Firstly, he could slow time. Then, he could call up all his energy and use it in a single attack. Both features of the Bridgeman clan. However, none of that explains him being unaffected by Elaine's attacks. It's like his body is automatically immune to all physical attacks. To beat him, I'll have to give it my all. I just hope that will be enough. Then, out of nowhere, Matej appeared.

"Congratulations" he said—"I heard you advanced to the finals."

"Yeah, but I am afraid of this Richard guy. He is a total mystery. He can slow time, and he isn't hurt by any of our attacks."

"I was right. He isn't a Bridgeman. And if what you say is true, if he doesn't get hurt by any attacks, he could really mean trouble." Matej wondered.

"But," I said "if he doesn't get hurt by physical attacks, we have to assume that he isn't hurt by our punches and kicks."

"And assuming that's true" Matej continued—"how can we beat him?"

"We? You aren't the one fighting him tomorrow in front of everyone, I am" I said.

Matej got an idea. I could tell by the surprised look on his face.

"What if he is of your clan?" Matej asked, snapping his fingers.

"I have considered that" I said "but I checked with grandma and others, and it doesn't seem like it."

I heard a noise just outside my house. I rushed to see it. It was a black cat. Just upon my sight of it, it vanished.

"What was that?" Matej said.

"I'm not sure . . . I replied.

Elsewhere . . .

"Update. Now. Revia" a mysterious voice said "is it all done?"

"Yes, it seems Martin Kelemen is getting ready for tomorrow. Should we move to capture him?" said this "Revia."

"No" the voice replied "we will get him after everyone else. He is not important. He is only a backup plan, remember that."

"Yes, sir." he replied.

"On my end, the Brightless have gone off the radar." a crooked voice said.

"Wonder why . . . Anyway, that doesn't matter. Anything else?" the voice said.

"With all due respect sir, it does seem that the Brightless society is plotting something big. Shall we proceed to attack them?" said a young, innocent voice.

"No, my brother will counter, and who knows what will happen then." the leader replied.

"And" the crooked voice started speaking again "I've got an informant saying that Damaken's king, Honorable Lord Goruhei, has died, and the new king is some Sebastian fellow."

"Very well. Let us pray."

"Just a minute" the innocent voice started speaking again "I've got some news."

"Spill it."

"It looks like Mixmaster's legacy's time has come. But what if he survives?"

"Do you doubt my predecessor's abilities, Turno?" the leader raised his voice.

"No, I'm sorry, sir." Turno bowed his head down to apologize.

Chapter 6

The Final Round

"Welcome everyone! Today, Martin Kelemen will fight Richard Trotten in an all-or-nothing stand-off. Well, without further adieu, let us begin!"

"Do you possess the Kelemen swords? Richard asked, right off the bat.

"I do not see what this has to do with our battle" I replied.

"So that's a no. Good. Then there's a 0% chance of success for you."

I charged at him.

"Bridgeman: Imperial Time Stop x 100!" he said.

Time was a lot slower, but I was still fast enough to punch him in stomach, hard. I had a lot of practice with Matej when it comes to countering the Bridgeman Imperial Time Stop. You just have to move in without thinking, follow your instincts, but you have to do that fast.

After a combo of hits, I moved in to finish him, charged my arm with lightning, and pierced his body.

"Is that it? Now I can finally kill you," he said. These Trotten siblings are all about killing. Though I can't see Lettie or Zannibi, I'm sure they're around here somewhere. The spoiled kids would never miss their "killer" getting his ass kicked by no other than their brother. Richard then took off his shirt, and revealed six lip-like things implanted in his skin. I couldn't move. I was paralyzed, like with Anne, only this time my opponent called up all his energy and fired it at me. I managed to break out of the paralysis, called Neron in the last second and got away scot-free. I then return called Neron, and backed away from Richard. My paralysis was undone; it appears to have been a visual illusion that happened upon seeing the lip-like things implanted in Richard's skin.

I could pull off a Plasma Bolt, but it probably wouldn't hurt him.

"DIE!" he screamed like a frustrated lunatic, as all his lip-like things on his body generated energy, which he then used to attack me. After the blast was fired, a look of surprise and terror appeared on Matej's face.

And that's when I noticed. Something felt different. My arms had gotten heavier. Could it be that I had acquired the Kelemen swords? I threw a lightning bomb and evaded Richard's attack. The attack was faster than others, but I was still faster. I tried to control the newly-found dense molecules that made my arm heavier. I just hardened my arms as hard as I could, and two majestic, iron black swords came out. They were still partially in my arms, and I couldn't get them fully out. It hurt like hell.

"Kelemen Seal" his body was starting to be sealed in my swords, after I had stabbed him. Just before I sealed him, he gave up, so I won the match. He returned to the watching arena, and did not stay sealed in my swords. Hadn't he given up on time though, who knows what would've happened. My swords were unmarked (empty), with no one sealed in them yet. I stayed in the fighting arena as the Mighty Shield deactivated.

"The winner of our 14th annual 7th Grader's Interschool Tournament is Martin Killman Kelemen!" the announcer said.

"Killman!" everybody cheered. Everyone from my class made a circle around me.

I was so happy. Happiness. Something I haven't felt in a long time.

"Let's all go to Elydorf's! My treat!" Barney said. Elaine smiled at his selfless announcement. Barney smiled back.

"You guys go on, I'll catch up" I said.

"Okay, but you better be there!" Max smiled.

"How could I miss it?" I smiled back.

An awful lot of both smiling and happiness. And yet another title for St. Atlas. It's a great day.

I saw Matej talking to Richard.

"Freak" he said—"who are you? What are you?"

"Nobody. Absolutely nobody." Richard responded.

"I'm not letting you get away" Matej threatened.

Then, Matej fell unconscious. He quickly regained consciousness, but when he did, Richard had already fled the scene.

"So, I guess we're still in the dark in the whole 'Who is he' thing?" I asked Matej, as I appeared behind him.

"Yes" he answered "but congratulations on the victory!"

"Thanks" I said.

He disappeared. I went on to meet my friends at Elydorf's, when I saw her. She was . . . I can't even begin to describe her. Blond, bright-orange hair, brown eyes, more beautiful than Elaine's, and a really beautiful and cute face. It was love at first sight. I mean, for me. Then she looked at me, while I was looking at her, and she smiled. That pure-hearted smile, the prettiest one I had ever seen. I just wanted to kiss her so badly. She was with some friends that looked like sixth graders, so I think she is a sixth grader, one year younger than me.

After she escaped my sight, I ran to catch up with my friends. We had fun the whole night and then, around 12 p.m., we went to sleep.

"You did a good job" one of my best friends, Proshko, said, as we were leaving Elydorf's.

"Thanks" I replied.

CHAPTER 7

THE WOLF

"I think we should redecorate the lobby. I mean the guests want to see the OSW castle as an entertainment training environment, not as some idiotic, ugly society." David said, a member of OSW. We were in a meeting. They take place twice a week, on Tuesdays and Thursdays.

"Yes, and then they could see the horror of our training. I agree with David," Phil said, his Anena.

We debated for a long time, and then decided for a redecoration of the main room and the lobby. Moments after we came to our decision, the alarm went off.

"There you are."

All of us turned our heads at the same time, and saw him. It was James Wollftreig. He is a member of the Brightless society, a society that is a sworn opponent of the OSW.

"Dave and Phil, cover my right. Bridgeman and Kelemen, left. Angel and Claire, cover my back. And Alice, be ready" said Katarina.

James was a werewolf, of the werewolf Wollftreig clan, with exceptional strength, and impressive speed. His grey, bloodshot eyes, grey fur, and long, white fangs intimidated his opponents.

"Ryunichi: Calling: All my exes!" Katarina started. Suddenly, about 50 male vampires appeared from the ground. They all charged at Wollftreig, and he started tearing them all apart like paper.

Then, the air around Alice suddenly shifted. She was of the Firod clan, and could call her guardian spirit, the Tannimi. She called Tannimi, and Tannimi hit Wollftreig with her right arm. He did a back spring, and returned to his original position, somewhat wounded.

"Trueearth: Cagebird!" David shouted, trapping Wollftreig in an earth cage. Wollftreig quickly destroyed the cage, finished off the last of Katarina's exes, and charged at Alice, and even after Tannimi protected her and repelled Wollftreig, he changed the direction and attacked Matej.

"Bridgeman: Imperial Time Stop x 100" Matej said.

Time slowed, and I threw 5 lightning bombs at Wollftreig.

"Piranha Sea!" Matej continued, as Wollftreig fell into a newly created pool full of piranhas. I then detonated my lightning bombs, which caused Wollftreig to be electrocuted in water, thus killing an ordinary man. However, James Wollftreig was no ordinary man. He jumped out of there, angry.

"I'M GONNA KILL YOU!" he screamed as he ran straight ahead to kill Phil.

"Pentoline: Hair Trap!" Katarina said, trapping Wollftreig in her extended, 5 m long hair.

"Kontetti Tire Out!" Phil said, as green laser rays attacked Wollftreig.

Kontetti are green lasers that one can command. They can form any shape one wants, and once you get hit by a kontetti laser, it feels as though you were hit by a bullet, and the damage done to your body is as if you were hit by a bullet as well, if the kontetti wielder shots one ray.

Phil shot 200.

Alice then rushed to the now very weakened Wollftreig and Tannimi tried to rip his head off, but he freed himself from Katarina's hair, and knocked Tannimi out. Now Alice needed to wait for half an hour before she could call her guardian again. Wollftreig attacked me, but Claire called her horse, and it knocked Wollftreig out of the way. He then got back on his feet, and David attacked him with earth needles. He barely got out of the way when Matej slowed time again. I threw a lightning bomb, and, using her hair, Katarina threw him out of the window. I detonated my lightning bomb while he was in midair, and as he was falling outside of our castle, David sprung a giant needle out of the earth, which Wollftreig then landed on. At the same time, Matej sprung a giant water needle, which Wollftreig also landed on.

"It seems he is dead." Claire said.

"One less for the Brightless" Dave added.

We then went each to our respective homes.

At Brightless society's headquarters . . . .

"It seems that Wollftreig failed the assignment that we gave him." the obvious leader of the Brightless society said.

"Don't worry, Ver, I'll get them. Tomorrow I'll attack St. Atlas." an average heighted, somewhat chubby guy announced.

"Alright then. We start the terrorization with Kelemen. See you after he's dead." the leader concluded the meeting.

CHAPTER 8

ST. ATLAS UNDER ATTACK

I woke up today with an awkward feeling. I couldn't help thinking I was going to be attacked. Of course, the non-superstitious man I am, I thought it was silly and ignored it. I then went to school. "We have a fire element test today, I have to study," I thought on my way to school. I saw Barney halfway there.

"Hey idiot! Wait!" I shouted, and I rushed to him. When I got close to him he asked me if I had studied for the fire element test. "No" I responded—"I didn't. But I'm going to pass, at least I hope." We also had a practical part of the exam, it tested our fire attacks. When we got to school, we immediately had to go to class to take the test. After doing so, it was time for the practical exam. All quite routine, though this time we were expecting a harder test, considering it's the first test of our 7th grade. "Elaine Enrik" the fire tech said—"you're up first. Demonstrate a fire attack that would protect you."

"Fire: Double claws!" Elaine said as fire shielded her, like two giant shrimp claws.

"That's an A. Next is Proshko."

This went on for two more hours. We all got grades (of course I got an A, though Barney got a C) and then went to the hall. It was recess. Everything is ordinary today, and I thought it would continue in that fashion for the rest of the day. But then, a suspicious man entered the school. He wore the robes of the Brightless society, but their code prevents them from attacking institutions for an individual. It seems they really are desperate. I casually walk towards him, but before I got to him, he rushed down the stairs. I followed him. About 5 minutes of running as far as possible from the school, I caught up. It's better this way, this is my fight, not St. Atlas'.

"My name is Beoyun, and I will be the one who finishes you off!" he said as he threw a dynamite at me. I countered with my lightning bomb. The two exploded in midair. He ran to me and tried to hit me. I dodged, and kicked him in his stomach. Then, a bomb in his body went off. It was an illusion of him, so it didn't the real hurt him, but the damage was real to me. The good old illusion trick. Should've seen that one coming. I was saved because of my OSW Anena: Regeneration. It enabled me to regenerate, even after being blown apart. It's simpler than it looks; the unbreakable strings emerging from my Anena seal on my neck reattach every part of my body, they return every drop of blood to my body. The only way to counter it is to stop my heart before I can regenerate. It's quite easy once you catch me. Which he won't. Not to mention if I ever find myself in mortal danger, Matej will teleport through our Anena seals, and come to my aid.

"As I thought," Beoyun said—"it won't hurt you. So I'll just blow this place up. Self detonation: Maxima Nuclear attack!"

That idiot detonated himself. Ah, the brightness of the Brightless. Matej came since I almost died, so he slowed time and the before the bomb went off, managed to freeze the bomb's inner workings and throw it as far away as he could. Beoyun exploded in the air. It was quite an admirable blast, though not admirable enough. God I love fireworks.

"Another one less for the Brightless." Matej said.

We returned to the OSW headquarters, and reported everything to our fellow members.

"Okay, but there is a more important matter we should attend to. I finally found out who's the leader of the Brightless society. You're not gonna like it. It's Uncle Verbringer," Phil said, being the head of intelligence at OSW. None of us could hide our shock. The Uncle clan was a group of people adopted by a mogul simply referred to as "The Uncle". Each of his "kids" were stronger than even the headmasters of schools. However, I thought they were extinct. I thought Voyi killed them all. Never imagined there was a survivor.

"So what now?" Alice asked. "How can we win against him???"

"We will get there, and when we do, I'm sure we'll do great. Especially since now it's time for us to strike back. It's time for the Killhunt." David said.

Let me explain. The Killhunt is a process in which we of the OSW hunt down and kill members of the Brightless society. Since they're stronger, two Anenas will attack a single Brightless.

"It begins tomorrow. You better rest." David added, bringing our meeting to an end early, and, unfortunately, not letting Matej and I enjoy our fame for killing Beoyun.

CHAPTER 9

THE KILLHUNT

When I woke up, I went to the OSW castle. Matej and I were given Lady Insect in our Killhunt. She is a biological experiment. She can turn into an insect, and manipulate plants and insects around her. We were informed she would be at the Deathtower, so we headed there. As we traveled, Matej said: "How do you plan on battling her, with your entomophobia?"

"I'll endure, I guess." I replied. Yeah right. I'll be scared like I've never been scared before once we encounter her insects.

We arrived.

"Show yourself, freak!" Matej shouted. Not a great way to start a battle with an insect manipulator.

"Well if it isn't the Bridgeman failure and pretty boy" a voice came out of nowhere.

It was her. Lady Insect. Matej looked at her angrily.

"Insect, we have come here in order to kill you." I said, keeping some of the respect I had towards older people before I joined OSW. In this case, 12 years older.

"We'll see about that" she responded quickly.

"Total Insect Transformation!" she said, very loudly.

Her outward appearance changed. From a long green haired medium height girl, she went to a spiderlike creature, with spider legs growing out of her body, and with many other insect features, such as caterpillar skin. Her eyes went from blood red to orange (all very strange) and she seemed more merciless.

"No holding back, eh?" Matej said, with a fair amount of fear in his words.

"Total Insect: Poison Ivy Tackle!" she screamed.

Suddenly, out of nowhere, numerous ivy plant stems attacked us.

"Bridgeman: Imperial Time Stop x 100!" Matej shouted.

I shot a few lightning bombs at Lady Insect, but she protected herself with oak stem. Even with Matej's Imperial Time Stop, she managed to defend. This is gonna be hard.

"Iceberg Spike!" Matej said "Total Insect: Test Speed!" she interrupted him. As Matej's spike appeared from the ground, Lady Insect wrapped her ivy stabs around her arms, and used them to multiply her speed, launching her towards Matej, breaking his iceberg.

"Total Insect: Sticky Web!"

"Bridgeman: Imperial Time S" Matej shut up as Lady Insect's web wrapped around him. One way to finish this.

"Calling: Kelemen Swords!" I shouted. There was really no need for me to shout that, but I wanted to brag about my new possession.

"Oh no you don't! Total Insect: Spider Beatdown!" she shouted. Doesn't she ever let her guard down?

For the next 10 seconds, I was getting beaten up by her grotesque spider legs. I dropped my swords, which were partially separated from my arms before I dropped them. After she finished beating me up, she took out a blade and tried to cut my throat.

"Holtow: Leg Bounce!" I said, as both my legs hit her. Now Holtow is a fighting style that resembles a dance, leaving an opponent disabled, hitting all the vital points of a body. She was thrown away from me, but had quickly bounced back on her feet.

"Is that all? Can I FINALLY kill you?!" she screamed. "Total Insect: Katashina!"

Suddenly, out of the ground appeared tons of plant stems and before you knew it we were in a gigantic prison made of plant stems. Better than the stems wrapping around our bodies and breaking our bones, I guess.

"So what happens now?" Matej asked.

"Now we do this right. Lightning Bomb Barrage!"

"Waterfall Destruction!" Matej added. Both Matej's giant waterfall and my 12 consecutive bombs made out of lightning aimed at the back of the prison, its structural weak point.

But there had been no effect on the prison.

"Now! Die!" she said, as the stems grew closer to our bodies. The prison shrunk. They're going to crush us. C'mon, think! We have to get out of this somehow!

"Hey, Martin! I'll slow time as you use your school's signature attack to destroy this prison." Matej said.

Brilliant. I'll survive long enough to charge it because of the Imperial Time Stop, and since its purpose is to tear through anything that can't be torn because of magic, or in this case manipulation, St. Atlas' Khadun will easily save our asses.

"Let's give it a shot." I replied, after thinking it through.

"Imperial Time Stop x 100!"

"Here it comes! St. Atlas's signature shot! Attack of Khadun!" I shouted.

I charged my hand with red lightning, in a shape of a dragon, and I started cutting through the stem.

"You'll never take us alive!" I yelled.

"You idiot! I am LADY INSECT of The Honorable Brightless Society! I won't be taken down by mere children!"

I destroyed the prison and attacked her, but she managed to defend herself with more stem. The red lightning vanished; I didn't have the energy to keep it up. I would have done the Plasma Bolt, but I didn't have enough energy left for that either. Matej and I both backed down and fell down near a wall. We barely managed to get up.

"Unbelievable" she said "for someone to survive my Katashina . . . very remarkable. But it all ends here.

Total Insect: (I can't BELIEVE she still has energy left) Attack of cockroaches!!"

You guessed it. About a thousand cockroaches emerged from the ground. Ok, now we're done for.

"Water: Double Hanxle!" Matej yelled.

A hanxle is a giant arm with fangs, composed out of water. With two of those Matej attacked Lady Insect.

She tried to defend, but he slowed time. Still she managed to barely defend, and Matej's hanxle turned into water, and that water fell to the ground. He then used that water to bring my Kelemen Swords back to me, and I quickly took them and stabbed Lady Insect in her heart, with both my swords. I then sealed her inside my swords. Both Matej and I used the last of our energy to retreat to the OSW castle. David awaited us there. Now we'll rest and just wait for others to kill their targets. And then the Killhunt is over.

CHAPTER 10

ANOTHER TOURNAMENT

"How could you do that? He is your friend! Do you even know what you've done?!?" tech Jennsy shouted at a somewhat short, dark-brown haired young man.

"I didn't do that much damage." Mark responded.

"You . . . do you even know what "friend" means?"

"Yes. A friend is one that helps another friend in any situation, no matter the circumstances." Mark explained the word to his class-mistress.

"Enough of this. You don't deserve to call yourself a warrior." tech Jennsy said as she left. She was very strict when it came to rules and regulations of St. Atlas.

Mark Enrik was a disturbed young child. Ever since Kelemendawn, he began acting different and started having more of an evil presence. This resulted in him wounding a fellow classman. Either that, or he really pissed him off. Mark is a fifth grader, so he needs a mentor for his upcoming junior tournament. Normally, it would be his sister Elaine. But considering the fact he needs to be "controlled", that role has been passed on to me. Barney would've been a much better choice, considering that he's a much better, kinder person than I am. But no, Elaine just had to pick me.

"So, kid, I will be your teacher. I will put you through hell." I said. He didn't even look me in the eye. Not only have I threatened him, but I also let him know that I treat him as a child. A great way to start a teacher-student bond. The day I got my swords, my grandma sealed an Enrik in my swords. So now besides the "LI" mark on my left sword, I also have the "E" mark on my right one. Enrik's second strongest detector—Jo-Halaya Enrik.

"Now, kid. I'm here to make you the strongest warrior ever, after me, of course." I said, acting like a tough teacher. Seriously, I should've practiced at home in front of a mirror or something before ending up like a total pain in the ass.

"Why do you say that? Do you honestly believe you're the strongest? If you were, YOU wouldn't be here teaching ME" he responded rudely.

So much about that. Cocky little badger.

I backed away from him.

"Enrik: Deathbomb!"

I gathered all my Enrik energy into my fist and threw the energy towards a ravaged area, 3'o'clock, about 200 m away from me. The energy's power destroyed almost all the surroundings.

"Wow-w" he said.

"This is the strongest Enrik attack"

"The Deathbomb." he interrupted me.

Looks like I finally got to him.

"After you finish training with me, you will be able to perform that move."

"Fine" he said, accepting his place as my student. Not very thrilled, at least he wasn't showing it.

"Let's get to it, shall we?"

And trained we did, for a week, until it was time for Mark's tournament.

We (the 7th graders) need to take our places in the watching arena to observe our students (the 5th graders) battle each other. I didn't get a teacher when I was a 5th grader because there wasn't enough 7th graders to cover my whole generation, so the weakest would get laid off the program.

Mark easily beat his opponents using his earth attacks, and his Enrik techniques. But now it was his turn to battle Ivan Pornut, son of tech Nevilla Pornut (the water element control teacher), mentored by Fairchild Alpha, my rival who is said to be the strongest of our generation.

Fairchild is a blond haired brown-eyed guy, goes to 7. B (corresponding my 7. C), and excels in water attacks.

He, however, did not appear in the 7th graders tournament, due to him being in the hospital during the time. The idiot tried to prove some sorta theory and burned himself badly in doing so. Rumor is he still has flash burns on his chest. He's also the heir to the Vassnyan blade, an "almighty" blade that is rumored to control water. Anyhow, he suddenly appeared next to me in the watching arena.

"Martin" he said "your protégé will definitely lose."

"What makes you think that? I responded.

"Because Ivan trained under the world's most famous water element users. And Mark was trained ONLY by you." he said, full of confidence, with his superior voice that I'm so accustomed to.

"Well, I've put Mark through hell."

"We'll see who's better." he smiled.

"I guess we will." I responded.

Ivan is basically Fairchild Jr.; his garb, stance, hair and eyes are the same as Fairchild's. And from what I've heard, he is just as cocky.

"For the final match, Ivan Pornut vs. Mark Enrik—Begin!"

"I'll start" Ivan said "Giant Water Wave!"

A giant water wave emerged, and started flooding the arena. Impressive. Ivan intends to flood the arena, because he can manipulate water, unlike Mark, and thus save his part of the fighting arena from being flooded.

"Enrik: Giant Push!" Mark shouted.

A force repelled Ivan's wave, sending it to the back to him. Ivan then separated the water, so that he would not get hit.

"Double Water Tiger" Ivan continued, now having little more than half his energy left.

Suddenly, two gigantic tigers (made out of all the water Ivan had separated) attacked Mark. Mark glided in beneath one of the tigers and performed an Enrik Heart Stop, which caused the water tiger to explode, after which Mark continued to move towards Ivan. He attacked him with a few Enrik attacks, but Ivan defended himself with water.

"Enrik: Heart Stop Barrage!" Mark shouted while hitting Ivan multiple times with his Enrik energy, and once Ivan's water couldn't defend him, Ivan used his water shield to defend himself. The water shield, much like the earth armor, is a suit of water wrapped around a person in a body like shape, so that every time you take damage, a part of the shield will take the damage instead of you. That shield can regenerate itself, multiple times over. The only difference between Ivan's water shield and Mark's earth armor is that Ivan is surrounded by water (though it can become ice), while Mark is with surrounded by earth.

"Water rope!" Ivan shouted, as he created a rope made out of water. He threw it like a lasso and caught Mark in it. Mark got captured (he was not able to use his earth element attacks because Ivan would just counter them with his water), and that water tiger (the one that Mark didn't attack) charged straight at Mark.

"Enrik Shield!" Mark said as a shield of energy formed around him, destroying the tiger, and the rope. Mark returned to his original position.

"Got only one way to do this" Mark said as he was getting into the Deathbomb stance.

"Enrik: Deathbomb!" Mark said, throwing the Deathbomb at Ivan. It hit home.

As the smoke caused by the explosion cleared, it I could clearly see that Ivan was still standing.

"How impressive" I said "that he managed to use the combined might of all his energy and all his water to defend against the Deathbomb."

"Told ya he's stronger" Fairchild said.

Ivan rushed to Mark in order to behead him.

It was then I remembered the time I used to train Mark.

"Ok, you're all set!" I said.

"But before your training is finished, I would like to teach you something. There is a reason why I wanted to train you, other than that I was assigned to you, and that you're an Enrik. It's your malicious personality. And that's why I think this transformation will be most suitable for you. It's easier for you to control, though it's still hard. Oh, and be careful with it, or it will consume you. Get it?"

"Got it," he answered.

Back to the present.

"Damaken: Release!" Mark said, as his body became much like mine after using Damaken. His middle length brown hair turned dark, his eyes became black, and he was, like me, surrounded by a malicious dark aura. Explains the name: Damaken—Dark Magic.

"Damaken: Soul Dunk!" Mark said, charging at Ivan. He pulled Ivan's soul out of him, and slammed it in the ground.

"Game over" he said.

"The winner is Mark Enrik!" the announcer declared. Elaine clapped almost as hard as me, when she gave me that look. That "I'm glad you exist in my life" look.

Chapter 11

The Combination Training

The footsteps of an 8th grader whose name I later found out was Crowley echoed throughout the hall so loudly even our cabinet, nicely equipped with soundproof walls and all, could hear them quite clearly.

His 14 year old muscular body entered our classroom.

"Tech Mariah, the headmistress wishes to have your signature on this." he said, swiftly walking towards the desk where tech Mariah was, and handed her a bundle of white papers.

"I see." the Tech said, carefully reading the first few lines with the help of her black-framed glasses.

She then signed the papers, at which point Crowley took them and exited our classroom.

"What happened?" Elaine asked.

"Now we get back to what I was teaching." the tech ignored Elaine's curiosity, and continued explaining to us the basics of combination, including the making of the combination warrior. Matej and I could make a combination warrior, but through our Anena seals, and this was a class to teach us to combine without any seals, therefore making the combination warrior more diverse, independent, and ultimately stronger.

"I am going to guide you through this so that you can learn the true values of comradeship and combining forces."

Whoa, wait a minute. Nobody said we were gonna combine. This was all supposed to be in theory.

"So, to start with, each one of you will be given a white sheet of paper. It will glow when you find another warrior from this class that can combine with you." tech Mariah gave everyone their sheet.

"Kontetti: Combination Field!" she shouted.

Suddenly, a field of kontetti appeared, only it was blue (contrary to the usual green lasers). Although the landscape was quite impressive, nothing happened. Everyone just looked at their respective sheets, but no glow.

Then, after a while, two sheets started glowing.

You guessed it. One of them was mine. But the other wasn't Barney's nor Proshko's. Not even Neven's. It couldn't have been Elaine's, because guys cannot combine with girls. It was Johnny's. Now Johnny is from the Vlayer clan. He is a sword master, being able to wield the Vlayer swords. Technically, the Vlayer carry blades, making them the only one out of 5 sword master clans not to wield actual swords. The Vlayer blades are two sword-like blades with medium-sized holes in them (strictly for decoration). They are connected with a rope (which can be detached), and are very firm, almost impossible to break. Also, they can combine to create a spear.

Johnny is a short brown-haired, green-eyed guy, average height, has two sword holders on his back (like all sword masters), and the rope, which he uses to connect his blades tied around his waist, like a belt. On his right shoulder there is a tattoo, the trademark of the Vlayer clan. It's a cat with a dead dog beneath it. It represents the change in the role of the predator.

"So, basically, I have to combine with Johnny? How do I do that?" I said.

"Yeah" Johnny continued "I have no idea how to combine with Killman."

"Everyone but Vlayer and Kelemen! Class dismissed!" tech Mariah said. Everyone walked out of the class with great ease and a little concern for the two of us, not to mention an unimaginable level of curiosity, and only the three of us remained. Tech decreased the size of the blue kontetti field, and exited it, with it now surrounding only surrounding Johnny and I.

"You have to figure out how to combine on your own." tech Mariah said on her way out,

Great. She left us here alone. Now Johnny and I have to combine. And we have no idea how to do that.

"Are you as clueless as I am?" I asked Johnny.

"Even more clueless." he responded.

We then battled for about half an hour. He is some sword master. I heard a knock. It was tech Snorzy. And her class, 6. B. I recognized Robert and Bainbridge. That girl I saw after my match with Richard was there too. I looked at her closely. The veins on her left arm made an H-like shape, meaning that she is of the Hoopling clan, the Kontetti clan.

"Monica, why is that brown-eyed hottie staring at you?" a girl from her class loudly said.

"Shut up, Sarah! He is totally not!" Monica responded.

"Kelemen, Vlayer, I would like to use this cabinet for my Fahn class. Is that alright with you?" tech Snorzy asked.

"Yes." I replied.

"Same here." Johnny said.

"Okay then. Let us begin, class!" tech Snorzy said.

"Johnny" I said—"in order for the combining sheet to choose us, we had to have something in common. Think, what could it be?"

"I don't know. Let's keep fighting, maybe we'll detect the similarity."

After we took our shirts off, for combat's sake, of course, all the girls expressionlessly stared at us.

"So what now, genius?" I asked him.

"Don't ask me!"

That's when I realized why we could combine. The sheet chose us because we're both swordsmen.

"Get your swords out, Vlayer."

"Now you're talking!" Johnny smiled and took out his Vlayer swords out of his sword holder.

I ejected the Kelemen swords out of my arms. We attacked each other. As our swords clashed, a green ball appeared out of nowhere, repelling us to our original positions. It created another, red kontetti field around us, inside the blue one tech Mariah had placed us in beforehand. The field sparkled for a few seconds, then exploded. A harmless explosion of bright red light.

We combined. The combination warrior. I was now half of an average-length brown haired green-brown eyed guy. He likes to wear torn up clothes. As for his name? Vlayer and I agreed: Killvla. I am unaware of our combined power, but I am sure we will test it very soon. All of the 6th graders looked in shock and surprise as they saw Killvla go out the blue kontetti field. We quickly went to catch up with the rest of our class. They were in lightning class with tech Padyanna.

"Hey everyone." we said. Unfortunately, our voice is now deeper, more adult.

"Is this it? The combination warrior?" Jaden J shockingly said, surprised at the fact Johnny and I managed to pull it off.

"Smarter than Killman. More handsome than Vlayer. Stronger than the both. I am Killvla." we said. No one knew what to say.

"And his personality is even worse than that of Martin and Johnny combined." Elaine said, rolling her eyes.

"So this is what the combined warrior is all about." tech Padyanna said.

"Yep" we answered "now we just wait for a volunteer to test our might!"

"Class dismissed!" tech Padyanna said, afraid we'd destroy the place with this newfound power.

"Woo-hoo!" everybody shouted.

Without a moment to lose they all ran home. Killvla stayed in the school gym to practice his moves.

A few days later . . .

"So there he is . . ." Neven said. Swaltagar appeared. Four arms, spiderlike fingers, burned skin, short grey hair, brown-black eyes.

Neven, Proshko, Matthew and Michael stood guard and saw him. The four are supposed to guard the school tonight. I got the message from Matthew that the spider-freak had returned. Did tech Mariah knew Swaltagar was coming to our school? Is that why she taught us how to combine? All questions I don't have the answers for. Hopefully Swaltagar has. And hopefully we'll have to beat it out of him.

CHAPTER 12

KILLVLA VS. SWALTAGAR

"So you are the 7th grader brats guarding St. Atlas" Swaltagar said.

"Fang Capture!" Proshko shouted.

A giant beast's mouth emerged from the ground, trying to capture Swaltagar. He, however, escaped this imprisonment.

"Web Bullets!" Swaltagar responded to Proshko's attack, firing web cocoon bullets at Michael. Matthew called his giant's bat and repelled the web bullets.

"Motto Animal Adaption: Lion!" Michael said, adapting his body to that of a lion. He charged at Swaltagar, roaring.

"Calling: Spider Knives!" Swaltagar said, calling into battle his trademark organic knives made out of spider legs. He used two of his arms knocking the lion-adapted Michael up in the air, and the other two to stab him with 6 spider knives, but Proshko's Earth Element Body Blow Barrier managed to save Michael. The EEBBB (Earth Element Body Blow Barrier) is a shield which shields one animal, person, or being of any sort, and can be used even without looking, because the worms in the earth can sense the target. This was perfect considering that you couldn't see Swaltagar from Proshko's perspective, because lion-adapted Michael's body blocked the view. Matthew swung his giant's bat, aiming it at Swaltagar, but Swaltagar managed to dodge. Neven quickly turned into a ball and attacked Swaltagar. He couldn't dodge, so he used the spider web he spat out of his mouth to swing himself forward, therefore dodging Neven as a ball. Just before Neven hit the wall, Matthew swung his bat and repelled Neven, directing him directly to Swaltagar. He couldn't dodge, because Proshko had trapped him with his earth pillars. Swaltagar, however, stood calm. As Neven (curled up in a ball) hit him, Swaltagar countered with his fist. A fool's move, anyone would think. But it was far from it. Swaltagar's fist hit Neven so hard it knocked him back 12 m and reversed his transformation back to his normal self.

"Enough with the games" Swaltagar said, breaking free of Proshko's pillars. You could now easily see that Swaltagar's power was far beyond any of theirs.

"If strength is how you want to play it . . . fine by me! Motto Animal Adaption: Minotaur!" Michael said, as his body slowly started adapting to that of a minotaur.

"Total Malevolence" Swaltagar whispered, confidently grinning.

He soon found himself behind Neven, and hit him hard with four arms and two legs. Then he jumped in the air, and spat a giant spider web, big enough for him to use it as a field of movement. He reached the bottom, and came to Matthew, quickly breaking him down with hits. Proshko attacked Swaltagar with earth bridges, but Swaltagar dodged, broke Proshko's Earth Armor, and still knocked him away from the arena. Michael, fully transformed into a minotaur, attacked Swaltagar, but Swaltagar just pulled the giant spider web (from before) and trapped him. The web stole the minotaur-adapted Michael's energy, so he couldn't break free. When Michael's energy completely disappeared (he also returned to his normal form), Swaltagar undid the spider web, and knocked Michael unconscious, almost killing him in the process. He then took out a spiderlike sword and moved in to finish the job, with the first up being Neven.

"Royal Beheading" Swaltagar said, going behind Neven.

"This is the end for you!" Swaltagar shouted. It's amazing how almost every villain I have ever encountered is as much a cliché as any other bad guy. Then, a sound was heard. It was the breaking of Swaltagar's spider sword, done by the hands of Killvla's Killvla blades. The Killvla blades are a mixture of my Kelemen swords, and Johnny's Vlayer blades. They have various abilities, which we might need to use against the spider freak.

"Sorry we're late" he said.

"The combination, eh?" Swaltagar was quick to notice.

We looked around. Matthew lying helplessly on the floor with his calling ball beside him, Michael bleeding and knocked out cold, Proshko's Earth Armor broken, him injured, and Neven kneeling and staring at us.

"Die." Killvla said, as he teleported behind him.

"What speed!" Neven said, in a state of shock.

He took the Killvla blades and cut off all his arms, then returned to his original position. That Killvla is quite something.

"You! How dare you! I will kill you!" Swaltagar shouted, full of anger.

"Enough with the clichés, armless spider freak." he said as he connected the Killvla blades with the Vlayer rope, turning it into the Killvla Spear.

"Megabomb!" Swaltagar screamed sadistically, creating bomb shaped energy on his foot, then kicking it to us and Neven.

"Interdimensional transport!" he said, as a giant interdimensional hole appeared, and Swaltagar's bomb hit it. The bomb then went to another dimension. This is Killvla's power, opening up various dimension portals. Then, the hole opened up behind Swaltagar, and his own bomb hit him.

"Game over, idiot." he said. He then turned back to Johnny and I. We all headed to the infirmary, and after a few hours everyone was healed. Johnny and I were not combined anymore.

"What a day." Proshko said.

"Yeah" Michael added "who would've thought Swaltagar would be so strong."

"Well, it's all over now, and that's all that matters." Neven said, ending the conversation.

CHAPTER 13

THE DEADLIEST VILLAIN

It begun when tech Pornut detected an abnormality in the school's west wing.

"Pornut to Wendora! We have an intruder! Take care of the problem immediately, I'll come for backup as soon as I can" tech Pornut said, through the radio.

Tech Wendora quickly defeated the enemy so when tech Pornut arrived, it was already done, and the enemy was lying dead on the floor.

"Nevilla, that's . . ." said tech Wendora, talking to tech Pornut.

"Yeah . . . Ciara Bridgeman. But I thought she died in the raid of the Bridgeman clan." answered tech Pornut.

"She definitely did. On the dead body's front, there was an illustration. It was a large number "5". What could that mean?" tech Wendora said, wondering out loud.

"We should return to the teachers' lounge." tech Pornut said. Barney and I watched in anticipation and curiosity just like everyone else, wanting to know the story behind the battle.

And so they returned . . . just to see tech Snorzy and Mariah battling Muri Padyanna, original prodigy of the Padyanna clan, the LV1 lightning clan. However, with some effort, they managed to beat and kill him. He had the number "4" on him.

"Another person who should have been dead, yet is alive. Well, not anymore anyway. The numbers on the victims are very weird, though." tech Wendora said. Even with the reanimated deceased clansmen, the tech were all very surprised when out of the ground appeared Anyanna Hoopling, demanding someone stronger to fight her. This was the first corpse to speak. She had the number "3" on her front. The techs together managed to defeat and kill her as well, combining attacks of lightning, water, fire, earth, and wind. It was magnificent, really. Whoever this necromancer is, he obviously underestimated the power of the tech of St. Atlas. Anyway, I barely raised an eyebrow when observing the opponents, until the number "2" came. Darius Dan Enrik. The man responsible for Kelemendawn. He fought against all of the techs, and was beaten in the end, with the help of some 8th graders. I'm not that sure the techs needed the help, but Crowley and his team of muscular misfits sure like to pitch in. Finally, out of the earth emerged the mastermind. He had green skin, a very zombielike face, and constantly surrounded himself with plant stems, much like Lady Insect. Anyone could take one look at him and tell he's a necromancer, just like anyone could take one look at him and say his fighting is barely on the same level as that of a 6th grader.

"I am Lord Plant. I have gathered various warriors from the past, and I can call them to help me destroy this pitiful place. I have called four out of five, though they have done their purpose. You are all tired out, and thus can't even beat me, at your current state." Plant said. Oh, where to begin. Aren't necros supposed to be smart? Anyone here can beat Plant very easily.

"Begone with the tide!" tech Pornut moved her left arm to a 45 degrees angle, commanding a giant mass of water out of the ground to attack Plant. He defended with plants, but to no avail. He was barely alive when the attack ended. I'm surprised he thought he could defend himself against Pornut even more so than I am of the fact he defended himself with plants.

"We of St. Atlas will always defend our school! You can call all the dead warriors you want, break us until we cannot move, we will still hunt you down and kill you!" said tech Pornut. Unnecessary, but she was a rather theatrical woman. As she started yet another water element attack, the other techs got up and helped her. Then, they all shouted:

> "For the safety of the ones we love,
> For glory and the Mighty Lord above
> We will stand our ground and fight
> Until there is no more light;
> For the fallen ones never to see the light of day
> Respect St. Atlas's warrior way!"

They all bombarded Plant with super-strong continuous attacks. Plant remembered his youth. He remembered all the cheerful times he used to compete with his twin sister, all the times he had to prove himself, all of his contact with various insects which then became his pets, and thus his friends. He remembered the pain he felt when his parents were killed. After witnessing the death of his parents at hands of Uncle Tengu, he experimented on himself, to learn how to call dead warriors. Ultimately, these experiments took a toll on his physical appearance, however, he did become a necromancer through them. He managed to call up to five dead warriors. Each numerated from 5 to 1, from the weakest to the strongest. He wanted to rule the world, to enforce his laws, to make it his Battleworld, free of suffering. His plan was to use the warriors to destroy anything and everything in his way of conquering the world. And he wasn't about to let that go because some techs nearly killed him.

"Damn all of you! My plan . . . I wanted to rule the world! I wanted to be the best! It was all supposed to be mine!" Plant shouted. Such ambition.

"Don't be a crying little boy about it. You lose. Checkmate." tech Pornut said.

"No . . . I will die . . . but so will you! Take this—my trump card—

Now, before Plant finished what is his final calling, he thought, for a brief period of time, what consequences this attack will unleash. How the world he so much loved will suffer . . . the insects, the plants he once stood for . . . all gone. The forests all around the world he adored and took shelter in . . . burned to the ground. But even with those realizations, he still did it. Tech Wendora tried to stop it, but to no avail.

"My trump card—Calling!" he shouted, as huge black smoke appeared before him. The smoke cleared. Out of it emerged a warrior. He was a dark brown-haired guy. His looks and body were identical to mine. And now, Plant has unleashed a bomb that will kill us all. For the called warrior was none other than the greatest warrior of all time, one man who singlehandedly beat and eradicated the whole Uncle clan, the man who deserved the nickname "Wonderkid", always surprising and impressing both his parents and his mentors, one man who gave the terms "prodigy of the clan" and "genius" a whole new meaning; a man who had surpassed both his predecessors and superiors, and by teaching his inferiors quickly gained the title "teacher"—my older brother, Voyager Killman Kelemen.

CHAPTER 14

KELEMENDAWN

Voyager was a 16-year old boy at the time of his death. He was 11 years older than me. It all began one cold autumn day, few days after my fifth birthday. Voyager had just won the title of the strongest in his high school, the Honorable Kontetti School. This was the final drop for Darius Dan Enrik, an Enrik clan member who wanted the Enrik clan to be the best, to decide to sabotage Voyager. Darius thought and thought, until finally, he figured out the solution.

The Uncle clan. They were feared as the strongest. They are in fact a group of individuals with extra strong abilities, adopted by "The Uncle", who died after adopting the youngest, Uncle Alfons. Darius Dan gave Voyager's route from school to home and the time he will be there to the Uncles. There, the Uncle prodigy, Uncle 2410, was supposed to ambush him. Due to Voyager having To-Halaya Enrik in his Kelemen swords, he easily detected "the strongest Uncle ever". A battle emerged. This is later known as the bloodiest battle in the history of warriors. Uncle 2410 managed to extract and kill all but Mattea Hoopling from Voyager's Kelemen swords. In the end, 2410 died, and Voyager was badly injured. Almost out of energy, wounded, one eye blown up, cuts all over his

face and a fearful expression on his face. Then, out of
nowhere, all the remaining Uncles, except for Verbringer
and Alfons, who were on an assignment at that time,
arrived. 26 non-aging superhumans. At the same time,
my mother, father, sister and I had arrived to battle side-
by-side with Voyager. Even I, as young as I was, knew we
didn't stand a chance. If it were at all possible, I would've
been left at home. Uncle Mixmaster attacked Voyager. He
managed to dodge, but Mixmaster redirected his attack to
me. He used an eprouvette with some green-like thingy in
it and had made me swallow it.

"Because your little brother swallowed this, in eight
years' time, he's going to die." said Uncle Mixmaster,
talking to Voyager. His grin expressed his life perfectly; a
failed scientist who now exists only to hurt others. In my
case, very painfully.

Voyager saw me hurting inside already because of the
poison, and it made him extremely angry.

"Why are you doing this?" my police officer of a
father, said, hoping his pure heart will give him some
intel as to who's behind this.

"Easy"—Uncle Mixmaster said—"we are the best, not
some sixteen year old brat."

"But"—my father swiftly continued—"how did you
know he was going to be here?"

"You can thank your friend Darius Dan for that"
Mixmaster answered.

"Mother, father, sister, take brother with you and run!"
Voyager shouted.

"Are you insane? We have to help you, son!" dad
replied.

"I have already started the attack." Voyager replied,
interrupting our father.

Dad started crying. He quickly grabbed my mom, my sister and I, and got us away from there. I can still remember the look on his face when he knew he lost his firstborn . . .

"Heh"—Uncle Bendon laughed—"we will kill you and your family. Nothing can save you now!"

"This is it, Mattea. This is how far you are able to see, living in my swords. Ready?" Voyager said, talking to his ZESHB Kelemen sword. Only the H remained, though.

"Yes. Let's do this." Mattea said telepathically from his swords.

Voyager made a stance. He took a knife, and an image of Mattea Hoopling appeared behind him.

"This is nonsense"—Bendon said—"I will finish you off now!"

Bendon charged at Voyager. Just as his fist was about to hit him, Voyager emitted a kontetti field from his swords. It stopped Bendon's movements, and paralyzed all the Uncles. There is one special thing with the Hoopling: they have their veins in their left arm in a shape of a letter "H", symbolizing their clan. Their whole Kontetti power is stored there, in those 10 centimeters of glowing veins on the inside of their wrist. And Voyager had now gained that Hoopling feature, on his right arm.

"Hoopling: Bombarrada." Voyager and Mattea said at the same time. Voyager cut his H shaped veins, and that field of kontetti started exploding; lasers emerged from everywhere. It was the Bombarrada, a secret attack passed down in numerous forms only to the brightest Hoopling. And furthermore, Mattea was the only one alive who could actually do it. Every single Uncle there was killed. Voyager Kelemen died that day, hence the event came to be known as "Kelemendawn".

That night, after everyone heard what had happened to Voyager, I went to sleep. The rest of my clan decided to kill Darius Dan and to spare the rest of the Enrik, although we could've asked for the whole clan to be slaughtered. The normal and Dan divisions, that is. I then went to sleep, and that's when I dreamt of Voyager. I asked him why he did what he did. He said: "Because I love you. Always have and always will. I will continue to live, in your imagination . . . Succeed in the task I failed at. Bring laughter and joy to the world instead of fear and pain. Save anyone who needs to be saved. Become the strongest in my place. Because you of all people can do it, little brother. You have 8 years. 8 years is enough time. Be the hero I could never be. Be the hero this world needs so much."

I then woke up and cried all night . . . .

CHAPTER 15

THE MYSTERY WOMAN

"Huh. So this is the real world . . . how long has it been?" Voyager asked Plant.

"8 years. Now kill all of them!" Plant answered angrily.

"Or I could just kill you."

"W-What?" Plant mumbled in terror.

"Enrik: Heart Stop." Voyager said, killing Plant. He stopped his heart using Enrik energy.

"I detest using an attack developed by the elitist scumbag known as the Enrik, but let this be a demonstration to you all that although I wish no harm upon this world, I am no one's puppet. Just try to control me, see what happens. 8 years have passed . . . excuse me, but I have somewhere I need to be." he said, breaking a window with energy and busting through. Everyone thought of places he could've gone to, but nobody knew where or why.

I couldn't keep that shocked look off my face. I looked like I had seen true terror. Very few people here know that I am his brother, even fewer know he's mine. But the techs all know.

"I know this must be hard for you. But your brother isn't under Plant's control; he can do whatever the hell he wants." Barney said, trying to cheer me up.

"That's what I'm afraid of. Thanks to Mixmaster's loud mouth, Voyager knows that the Enrik are the ones who betrayed him. Which means . . ."—I started—"if he were to learn that the Enrik are alive, he would annihilate all of them." Elaine continued, sighing and trying to accept the possibility of a war.

"Voyager thinks I'm dead. He will be happy when he finds out I survived Mixmaster's poisoning. I can use that chance to stab him in the heart with my Kelemen swords." I said.

I can't believe I just said that. I hope it doesn't come to that. I hope my brother is still the hero I looked upon when I was a kid and that he hasn't become a vengeful sadist wanting to eliminate the Enrik once and for all.

"That's harsh, even for you. By the way, how did you survive?" Barney asked. Barney understood I kept the code of the warrior above everything else, even my emotions, when necessary. That's what Voyager taught me.

"Ryunichi: Blood transfusion. The blood in my body isn't mine. Mixmaster poisoned only my blood, not me." I said. Luckily, the Kelemen are one of the clans whose are powers passed on via DNA and brain matter, not blood.

"He thinks you're dead, so he's probably at the graveyard." Elaine very quickly concluded what so many others haven't been able to.

"I'll go with you. I'm not an Enrik, so I should be fine." Barney said.

"No"—I replied—"this is something I must do on my own."

I then left, headed for the graveyard. It was around 9 p.m., so the school was over, and thus no one was at risk. I trust the techs to have come with a plan in case I fail, or in any case in which Voyager remains alive. Though no necromancer is skilled enough to revive permanently. All I have to do is kill my recently revived older brother. Easy, except the fact that he killed the whole Uncle clan singlehandedly. As for the emotions, it's not as difficult as it seems, he's not my brother, he's just a reanimated corpse, an illusion, if you will, here for a very limited amount of time. Getting closer to the graveyard, I saw a shadow. I shouted: "Voyager", but there was no response. As I got closer to the person whose shadow pretty much scared me, I saw that he is a she. And she is rather interesting. Her face was covered by her scarf, and she had long, dark-brown hair falling on her shoulders. When I grabbed her by the arm and asked her who she was, she ran away. I tried to chase her, but she was faster than me. Unbelievable. I wasn't able to keep up. The OSW protégé not to be able to follow a person.

I then looked around and saw that there was no trace of Voyager. I wanted to go home, thinking he went there to see mum and dad, but I just couldn't bring myself to go anywhere. I stared at Voyager's gravestone for a few hours. I remember the young me thinking that his death was only a dream. That Uncle 2410 didn't turn against him. Then I remembered. The same day Voyager died I ran to a forest, scared of how my life would develop and who I would become, after I no longer had my older brother. While in the deep forest, I heard a girl cry. She was the same age as Voyager. I remember that they used to date, that he used to bring her home constantly, and that he entered the Honorable Kontetti School at the high school selection so that he could go with her. I never saw her again. The last time was when she walked my brother to school, several hours before he was killed. I then thought of Monica. Probably because this whole scenario was very scary. And nothing scares me more than asking Monica out. I am, of course, in love with her, although we have never actually talked. You know, with me being on the hit list of various bad guys and all. Something was telling me to go to the forest, the same one where I went the day my brother died. I went there, and I found his body. He was dead. HE was dead. I stood there, with an unseen look of shock on my face. I was sweating, shaking and almost crying. For the first time since I was five, I was afraid. Real FEAR. My brother, to "just" be taken out. I immediately thought of the girl who I saw at the graveyard. But no matter how strong she was, she couldn't have killed Voyager. He had four Kelemen swords, unheard of in the whole Kelemen clan. He had obtained people of almost every clan for his Kelemen swords. And he, like me, could turn into a vampire, and thus become immortal for that short period of time. There was no sun, so he could have done that. He was also Damaken, dark magic. But he STILL died. Unbelievable. His body very quickly disappeared; it evaporated right in front of me, just like all the other warriors Plant reanimated. The fact his body evaporated now means he died recently. I used an Enrik from my swords, Jo-Halaya, to detect any person in the vicinity, but no one was discovered. The killer had fled. This made me believe it was that girl, partially because she could flee so fast, and partially because she had visited Voyager's grave, prior to him being killed again. Means she also felt pain. I then returned home, did not tell anyone at home what had happened. I just told them I hadn't seen him and went to sleep. I woke up just before dawn, to see a woman standing near my bed.

"W-Who are you?" I asked, holding on tightly to my bed. I was petrified. I knew she was stronger than me, and I knew she came here for a reason.

"I am someone who you will hate. Someone who, in a now impossible future, you would love and care for. I will kill you next time we meet, and I can guarantee you it will be on the battlefield." she said and swiftly vanished. I tried to see where she went, but I couldn't. I thought it was all a dream, but unfortunately it wasn't . . .

And then came dawn. I was afraid, and still wondering about that mystery woman.

CHAPTER 16

MONICA HOOPLING

I woke up at 7 a.m. Barely had any sleep. Had decided that I will not think of last night. Did my hair, brushed my teeth, and then went to school. Classes pass quickly. And, after we were done, and she finally ditched her friends, it was finally time for me to meet her. Should I go with:

"Hey babe. The name's Martin K. Kelemen. What's your name, sweetie?"

Or maybe:

"Hi. I just lost a brother . . . again. Will you go out with me?"

Or even:

"I had always admired your beauty, and it is an honor to meet you, Monica."

Three very different approaches, yet all well within my range of expertise.

She saw me practicing my talk. She laughed.

Great, now she thinks I'm some sort of a creep.

I then approached her. I mean, I had nothing to lose.

"H-Hi. M-My n-name is Martin K-Killman Kelemen. W-What's yours?" I stuttered. Really? Me, stuttering.

This world really is coming to an end, if someone like myself is confused while meeting a girl. A 6th grader, at that.

"I'm Monica Mattea Hoopling. Nice to meet you." she said.

I was happy. SHE is glad to meet ME. I wanted to rub it in Barney's face, but he wasn't near me. Though I suspect he was keeping his distance, watching me . . .

"So, um"—I said idiotically with one hand over the other, in a number "4" position—"would you ever like to have a cup of coffee with me?"

"Umm . . . I don't really do coffee." she responded.

"Oh. W-What do you do?" I asked, again idiotically.

"Does it matter?" she asked.

"Kinda" I responded.

"Things that amuse me and have absolutely nothing to do with school." she answered clearly.

"And coffee does not amuse you?" I continued, and you guessed it, like an idiot.

"Maybe it will, if you're the one I'm having it with." she answered, winking at me.

I smiled.

"Great. Pick me up at eight?" she responded.

"I'd be glad to." I answered.

The fourth idiotic thing I had said that day. I then walked towards Barney and Elaine, who were laughing at me. They were eating chips. Barney was wearing sunglasses, and Elaine was wearing a colorful short-sleeved shirt. Great.

"It's not funny" I responded to their silly reaction.

"But it is!" Elaine responded.

"Barney, you wouldn't have done any better." I said.

"Hahaha! See!" Elaine added and Barney reacted with a grim face.

". . . and Elaine wouldn't have done much better either" I continued.

"Hey!" she said, angrily. We hung out some more, and then went home. I couldn't wait 'till 8. I spent two hours doing my hair. Seriously, who does that? I decided to ask Robert and Bainbridge, friends of Monica's for advice on both what should I do and her. But mainly advice as to handling her.

"Dude, she's freakin' retarded." Bainbridge said, responding to my inquiry regarding Monica. We were walking near the School of St. Atlas; I was walking them home after school. It was 6 p. m.

"And why is she retarded?" I asked.

"Because she can't do anything! She can only battle with kontetti, because of her being a Hoopling. Though if you ask me, she is a disgrace to the clan" he answered, shaking his head a bit.

"So was Mark Enrik." I responded.

"But Mark had all this hidden talent. She doesn't."

"How do you know?"

"Trust me. Don't waste your time on her . . . She's not her sister." he replied. I didn't know Monica had a sister.

"What do you mean?" I asked.

"Annette Hoopling was top of her class. Strongest Hoopling prodigy ever, always seeking out more power. When growing up near a person like that, you have very little self confidence." Robert said.

"You're right about that. So that's what it's like, huh . . . ." I said.

"She, however, is a great friend, and a great person . . . once you get to know her." he added.

"Which is soon. I should go. See you kids later." I said, full of enthusiasm, and ran home, while my mind was playing 10 different scenarios for how this night might end. And the rest is history.

CHAPTER 17

THE CLANHUNTERS

"Is all prepared?" the voice said. Yes, it was the same voice as before. Their leader.

"Yes, sir"—Revia obediently answered—"but are you sure you can beat someone like Voyager? He killed your whole clan, sir."

"I'm going, and I will come back with Voyager's body, extract people from his Kelemen swords, and bring us closer to accomplishing our goal. Avenging my no-good clan is just an added bonus I couldn't care less about. If you dislike that, I will, without the smallest hint of hesitation, kill you."

Quite the leader, this one.

"Sir, with all due respect, you couldn't." Revia answered.

"Enough of this! I'm going."

"See ya, boss!" all 4 of his fellow society members answered in unison.

Intel says they are the Clanhunters. They hunt any member of the ZESHB, the union of the 5 strongest clans (in order, from strongest to weakest):

1. Zynnick (excels in fire attacks and calling dragons.)

2. Enrik (focuses on destruction of the nervous system, therefore disabling the enemy, rupturing their organs, and decreasing both their stamina and their energy.) Also excels in earth attacks. This, interesting enough, is not a clan legacy; it's actually just a tradition of the Enrik.

3. Stodyanna. There are 4 lightning clans. Stodyanna is the strongest. They can call up to millions of volts. Other lightning clans are Padyanna, Radyanna and Quanna.

4. Hoopling. They use kontetti. Those green lasers can easily destroy one's body; especially since the Hoopling can create their "arena" and therefore create whatever they want with their green lasers. Center of their power is in their veins; they are in an "H" shaped position.

5. Bridgeman, who can not only can slow time, but can also call up all their energy to blast "The Strongest Attack", an energy ball strong enough to destroy 50 square meters of space.

The Clanhunters hunt members of ZESHB silently and efficiently, aiming to somehow extract their clan's potential. However, the Clanhunters can get all they want from a single Kelemen who has any one ZESHB member in his swords. And since their plan to hunt ZESHB has somehow fallen to pieces, they want Voyager now. Their superior intelligence resources probably told them my brother's been revived, so they are coming to kill him. But they don't know he's dead. Worst of all, we are hearing this now on a fire element class, and are asked to evacuate. "In case the bandits come through our school while obtaining their objective". Please, I know as well as the fire tech that the so-called "bandits" will come to St. Atlas for none other than me, once they learn Voyager is gone. At least they're keeping me safe.

Elaine and I decided to go to my house and talk about . . . well, nothing really. She came to my house after I rested for 3 hours.

"Hey" she said.

"Hey" I replied.

We went upstairs, started eating and drinking stuff, and talked about power. She thinks she's stronger than me, but she isn't. We argued about that all night. That is, until Mark joined the party.

"And what are you guys up to?" he said, immediately eating the giant bowl of chips on the table.

"Hey, annoying little brother." Elaine replied, wasting no time teasing Mark. She also mumbled something about her being stronger than him.

"Uh . . ."

"What was that, Martin?" Elaine asked very angrily.

"Nothing, nothing!" I quickly defended myself.

"He said "Uh . . .""

"Not helping, Mark!" I shouted at him.

"Come on, the two of you versus me. Right now. I dare you, come on!" Elaine shouted, trying to prove her might.

"If you're not stronger than me, how can you beat us both?" Mark and I said at the same time.

"Enrik: Heart Stop!" she said as she attacked us, not wasting any time. I barely dodged, using my own Enrik to detect the direct invisible path of the Enrik Heart Stop, and Mark blocked it with his Heart Stop.

It's amazing how large and spacious my training room is. I bet we could have a tag match here.

We fought for the next five minutes or so, when Elaine finally admitted defeat at the hands of us.

"Will you two Enrik now battle me?" I suggested.

"Or will it be 7th graders vs. 5th graders?" Elaine replied.

"Enrik versus you." Mark said.

"Fine by me" I replied.

Elaine smiled, like she was thinking "I'm totally gonna beat you" or something like that.

We then started our battle, but we had no idea what would come afterwards . . . something that will change our lives. Forever.

CHAPTER 18

UNCLE ALFONS

That day, Uncle Alfons, the leader of the Clanhunters, decided to attack St. Atlas, because he believed Voyager to be there. Alfons wanted to kill Voyager so that he could get all the power Voyager had by extracting Voyager's Kelemen swords, therefore imprisoning everyone and everything he had in his Kelemen swords, and storing it somewhere, or injecting himself with it. The techs should have awaited him there. The techs were indisposed. I don't know or wish to know how Alfons did it. He wanted to find and kill Voyager. When he finds out Voyager's dead, he will come for me. I'm sure of that. He came into the now empty St. Atlas, or so it seemed.

"Hmmm, it seems Voyager isn't here. So Plant messed up. Well then. Time to get out of here."

"That's not an option" a voice behind him said.

"Who's there?" Alfons said and turned around. But he saw no one. Nothing. Until a person appeared behind him, and punched him, knocking him 5 meters away.

"I don't care who or what you are, but you're not touching Martin." It was Barney. He knew full well just who and what Uncle Alfons was, not only because of the Buttons family's ties to the Uncles, but because I tell my best friend everything, and this crazy maniacal survivor wanting to kill me is not an exception.

"Huh" Alfons grinned.

"Uncle Energy Attack!" he said, as a ball of energy emitted from his hand. He threw the ball at Barney, but Barney dodged, and attacked Alfons.

"Time for a total beatdown!" Barney shouted, attacking Alfons.

"Uncle Energy Mega Blast" Alfons launched a giant energy wave at Barney.

His fearful eyes stared at the wave; his body started trembling. He knew he couldn't dodge the attack, nor take it head on and survive. Then, tears started emerging from Barney's eyes. He knew he'd reached the end of his young, unfulfilled life. He lived sadly, trying to be cool, so much that he'd sometimes hurt Elaine and me on a daily basis. But he loved us. I'm sure of that. And the thought of him loving Elaine ran through every inch of his body, as Alfons's attack devoured him from inside out. His body became merely trash; his brain became merely an empty mass, and he became merely a memory. When the attack ended, Barney's destroyed body hit the floor. It was his final stand. From that moment on, Barney Buttons was no more . . .

"That takes care of the trash." Alfons said, wiping his hands one at another.

"I couldn't agree more" another voice said.

"Who's-"

"Water Wave!" the voice interrupted him. And it was none other than the only person besides me and maybe Elaine that could even stand up to Alfons, the wonderkid of our generation: my archrival, Fairchild Alpha.

"Now that the trash is out"—Fairchild said—"will you attack someone who's way more powerful than poor Barney?"

"At least you'll prove more of a challenge. I hope you do, because I just love amusing myself." Alfons answered, smiling.

Alfons took some damage from the Water Wave, but he was still standing. Probably because he is a strong man, so a little water couldn't possibly hurt him.

"Time to start." Alfons said.

"Water Train" a giant train-shaped mass of water emerged from the ground and hit Alfons.

"Energy Wave" Alfons said as he fired an energy wave from his hand and destroyed Fairchild's train. The energy wave, however, combusted after destroying Fairchild's water.

"Cocoon of destruction!" Fairchild continued. A giant cocoon of water covered Alfons.

Alfons busted through with his energy attacks.

Both combatants were running out of energy, because both Fairchild's water and Alfons's energy have one special ability: they take energy upon impact. And a few energy rays hit Fairchild, just like masses of water hit Alfons. Energy-cutting Uncle energy and energy-cutting water. Now that's a battle.

"Got energy for only one more attack: Ultimate Uncle Energy Blast" Alfons shouted, charging his hand with energy; creating an energy sword.

"That makes two of us. Water Sword Of Vassnyan!" Fairchild responded to Alfons's attack, as a water sword formed in Fairchild's hand.

The two clashed. A clash of two stars: one so young, with hopes, dreams and expectations; the other with nothing left of his pathetic life, living only to fulfill his disturbed goal.

Crack.

They switched their original positions, both having a 16 cm wound across their chest.

"This . . . is it! It for you! You said . . . you would be a challenge! But look at you! Lying here, almost . . . dead!" Alfons shouted, in pain.

"I will die. But there will be another; one who will protect this generation better than I ever could." Fairchild responded, calmly smiling.

"And who might that . . . be?" Alfons asked.

"Martin Killman Kelemen." Fairchild responded cheerfully.

"Heh . . . I will die, and so will you . . . but my minions will come for Martin and kill him. Even if he is stronger than you, my servants will have no problem killing him" Alfons said, coughing up blood.

"No, no . . . that's not what I meant. Martin . . . is special. After what you've done to Barney, he will hunt down and kill every single Clanhunter. And, Alfons . . . shame I had to be killed by someone as insignificant as you." Fairchild said, taking his final breath, and laid helplessly on the floor, bleeding.

"Ditto." Alfons answered. He then fell on the floor, bled out, and died.

7th of October . . . the day that would come to be remembered as the day two warriors fell in a battle against evil . . . and the day I will come to remember as the one of the saddest days of my life. The techs came later on and called the families of the deceased, and only their families, expressing their grief. Then, Sunday ended. It was time for Monday, and for us to go to school once again, not aware of what had happened . . .

CHAPTER 19

K-TEAM

"No" I said. I refuse to accept the fact that he's gone. I refuse to accept the fact my best friend is dead.

"W-Why???" Elaine wondered, breaking down in tears.

She cried. And I mean really cried, the kind that makes you want to become a hero the world has never seen just so you can salvage your friends and acquaintances alike of it.

Proshko patted me on the back.

"I'm so sorry, Martin." he said. Not that he could've said anything else. After all, he and Barney were never the best of friends.

"There's nothing to be sorry about. He's not dead. I will not acknowledge it. Never." I responded, trying to keep myself from crying. Heavens, it's hard.

My best friend, the one person who has always been there for me, was no more; merely his memory remained . . .

We were excused from school because of this. It wasn't long till' Tuesday came, and I knew it was time for me to stop grieving. It was Barney and Fairchild's funeral.

Barnabus Charles Buttons was my best friend. He was the one person I could've trusted with anything; from my feelings towards Monica to my brother's destiny. He was the kind of person I would ask to be my best man. This mightn't be a big deal, but with us Kelemen, it is. We have a very, very, very strict code when it comes to anything that is even remotely connected to our wedding. Whether it's the bride, the reception itself, or the best man. They would never allow a non-ZESHB or a non-KVLES to be my best man. But I wouldn't care. I would make Barney my best man regardless of the clan's sanctions and restrictions. I loved Barney Buttons with all my heart. That's why I wasn't at his funeral.

And where was I? Assembling my dream team, of course.

First up, Matej Bridgeman. I have chosen him for countless reasons, the most important one being that I can work best with him.

Second up, Sebastian Varyabla. After Lord Goruhei died, 13 year-old Sebastian took his place as the leader of the Damaken society: its members being all Damaken users, including Mark and I. He will be most useful. After all, he is the king of dark magic.

Next up, Tommy Zynnick, my cousin. He can perform most of the Zynnick clan attacks, and is here because of his fire abilities.

Then, Alice Firod. Not only because she's OSW, but also because she can work well with Sebastian; Tannimi can easily complement with Damaken. Tag attacks are key to beating the Clanhunters.

Followed by: Mark Enrik. He's an Enrik. Works well with Monica Hoopling. She is my number six. Including me, there is seven of us, and our targets are the following:

Morto Citti: A Clanhunter capable of calling various knives and blades, and can handle them like a professional sword master.

Revia: a mysterious Clanhunter of which we have no knowledge of at all.

Turno: a Clanhunter that has the power of all clans he has absorbed thus far; he's like a living example of the Kelemen swords.

Wicked: a Clanhunter who is very hard to injure. And I mean very hard. He makes Proshko's earth armor seem like nothing.

But we had to make one more stop: St. Atlas. On the way to the 8th graders' cabinet, however, we encountered Elaine.

"Relax, I will not be hurt. I HAVE to do this. I just have to." I said, before she could say anything.

Her cute little face became sad; she was worried. Worried beyond belief.

And then, out of nowhere, she got angry.

"Then take me with you! Surely I won't be defeated!" she shouted, taking deep breaths.

"No, that's out of the question." I answered.

"What? You're such a hypocrite! I must let you go, but you can't let me go? You're not THAT much stronger, you know." she said, even angrier than before.

"Enrik: Heart Stop" Mark attacked Elaine. The attack hit her, not enough to hurt her, but just enough to prove to her that she is too weak to go with us. Or just let her believe that. The real reason I'm not bringing her is pretty obvious, though.

If she died, I would undoubtedly commit suicide.

We then proceeded to the 8th graders cabinet.

"Mimmy Yanter?" I asked a bunch of 8th graders.

"Yes?" Mimmy answered. She was a typical long brown haired hot girl. Nothing special about her, just like there's nothing special about her ability. But we need a close combat expert. Barney was one.

"Come outside." Bridgeman said.

"Okay . . ." she left the cabinet, very confused.

Everyone stared at us like we were from another world.

"May I be of any assistance?" she asked us.

"We just want to talk." Sebastian replied. Sebastian's looks scared most people, but not Mimmy. He was all dressed up in black; and had, like all Damaken, black eyeliner and makeup. The only difference is that he was Damaken in his neutral state; he didn't have to transform.

"Talk about what?" Mimmy answered, fiercely. She started to get a bit aggressive.

"We know your brother, Cadmer, is wanted because of his ability to remember anything he sees instantly. He really is one in a million, and that's why the Clanhunters want him. You did have a problem with them a while back, didn't you?" I asked her, intriguing.

"So what do you want? Alfons is dead, anyway . . ."

"Come with us. We are going to kill every last one of the Clanhunters." I said.

Now this was a hard decision for Mimmy. She wanted to go with us, but she was afraid because she didn't think her mere brute force would be enough. It wasn't, but she will be in our team. Combined, we are invincible.

"OK. But you all better be strong, alright?" she answered, hesitating. Matej chuckled.

Then, as we were going out of the school, I heard a girl shouting: "Take me with you!"

No, it wasn't Elaine. It was Lucy McSmarts. She goes to the same class as Monica (6th B) and excels in the chemicals, acids and all, because she's from the McSmarts clan.

"We could use her"—Monica said—"she does have impressive potions."

"Fine, but you better stay out of my way." I replied. Great. More responsibility. Like Mark isn't enough.

"Right . . ." she replied, irritated by my command.

That's when we left the school. The K-Team. A Zynnick, an Enrik, a Hoopling, a Bridgeman, a sword master, a necromancer, a chemist, a close combat expert, and a spiritual fighter.

"Ok guys, we'll split up. Sebastian and Alice, you go after Morto. He attacks with knives, which you are invulnerable to with Damaken and Tannimi. Mimmy and Tommy, you go after Turno. Zynnick is the strongest clan, and Mimmy's brute force will be useful against this one. Take him out in one blow. Also, take Lucy with you. The more, the merrier. Mark and Monica will battle Wicked. Time to see just how well the Enrik and the Hoopling work together. And finally, Matej and I will go after Revia, Alfons's replacement. Any questions?" I asked, after my somewhat long speech.

"No? Good. Scatter."

Alice and Sebastian first found Morto, after full 2 hours of searching. They weren't tired, though. Unlike the rest of us.

"And who might you be?" Morto asked.

Morto is a 25 year-old white haired blue-eyed guy. He looks smart and wise, full of knowledge, and probably is. Not that that's gonna help him.

"We are Sebastian and Alice of the K-Team and we are here to kill you." they answered simultaneously, without fear. Not that those two were ever afraid.

"Let's not waste any time then. Calling: Rain Of One Thousand Knives!" he shouted.

"That's a way to start a battle." Alice said, with a smile on her face.

"Tannimi, come!" she continued.

"Damaken: Black Shield!" Sebastian shouted, as a giant black shield appeared. It looked like one of those shields warriors had in medieval times. The shield repelled the knives, so Morto reverse called them.

"Tannimi! Slash!" Alice commanded her Tannimi to extend her right arm and attack Morto, which Tannimi did. He dodged, but the arm attacked him again, this time from the back. He dodged again, but he fell down; so when he got up, he got caught up in Sebastian's Damaken Kettner. The Damaken Kettner is basically a giant wave of dark energy attacking the victim's bones, resulting in the break of the collar bone and the disablement the victim's arms.

"Calling: Knife Parade!" Morto shouted, as he called various knives and fired them at Sebastian, nullifying his Damaken Kettner.

"Oh no you don't! Tannimi Force!" Alice said, making Tannimi create a cannon out of her right arm, and fire a wave full of purple energy.

"Calling: Giant's Tooth" Morto responded, ironically, calling a giant tooth into battle. He used it to reflect Tannimi's wave back at Alice. Tannimi shielded her, but then she disappeared, along with the giant white tooth. I guess the tooth's infected with magic, or something.

"Sebastian, I won't be able to use Tannimi for another half hour! Can you do without me?" she breathed heavily.

"Huh?" Alice continued.

"Sebastian, why is Morto not moving?" Alice asked, wondering, eyes like that of a baby when asking her mommy why she had come home early. Except with a helluva lot of fear.

"He's mine now. I've casted the strongest Damaken attack: Phobos and Deimos" Sebastian said.

"And . . . um . . . what's that?" Alice asked, very confused about Sebastian's attack.

"It's an attack that focuses on one's psyche. It practically freezes the body, and shows illusions of the victim's loved ones getting killed, and hurt. Hard to perform, but due to you constantly pursuing Morto, he had to stay calm this split second, while calling his tooth. This attack is unbreakable, unblockable, undodgeable. Morto's already done for."

"Right, um, so what now? I'm sorry, I forgot." Alice asked Sebastian, shamefully.

"We go to St. Atlas and wait for everybody there." he replied seriously.

"Ok. Let's go!" Alice replied cheerfully.

Elsewhere . . .

"You, the brunette, you're the weakest. Your punches barely hurt me. You, fatty, are a disgrace to the Zynnick clan. And you, blondie, cannot mix any chemicals correctly; but then again, all McSmarts are losers" Turno said, while battling Mimmy, Tommy, and Lucy.

"The only reason you can't feel my fists is because you're hiding in that pathetic Lightbomber shield, so I can't get to you!" Mimmy shouted.

"We aren't losers!" Lucy shouted, offended.

"You say that I'm a disgrace, but that's coming from a guy who steals the power of others." added Tommy.

"Like your precious little cousin?" Turno replied.

"I would like to see him in battle."

"There's a difference between Martin and you." Tommy continued.

"And what that might be?" Turno asked.

"My cousin would be able to dodge this." Tommy smiled.

"Dodge what?"

"Zynnick: Demi Overheat!" Tommy interrupted Turno.

The Demi Overheat was the second strongest Zynnick attack, and the strongest attack Tommy could perform. It used all of one's fire to heat up the bottom half of the person's body. Turno wasn't fast enough to intercept it. It trapped his bottom half, burning it in the process.

He screamed in pain.

"McSmarts: Neutralization Compound!" Lucy said, calling a chemical into battle and throwing it at Turno. It decreased his energy to zero upon contact. This chemical is powerful, but it's hard to hit. Luckily, Turno was trapped.

"Now that your energy is gone, no more Lightbomber shield. And that means—

"Kaboom!" Mimmy interrupted Tommy hitting Turno with all her might, which resulted in Turno's collar bone breaking in half; and him dying.

"Woo-hoo!" Mimmy shouted.

"What a sadist" Lucy rolled her eyes.

"Let's head back. We have to meet up with the others." Tommy said.

Elsewhere . . .

"What is this guy made of? None of my Hoopling attacks are working!" Monica shouted, frustrated. Monica was far from the clan's failure. She does have bad grades and all, but she is fairly strong. And I know Mark is extra strong. So why are they losing to a guy who can only punch and kick?

"Monica, get away. Enrik Damaken: Dark Deathbomb!" Mark shouted. Dark Deathbomb. Only other person able to perform this attack was my brother.

The Deathbomb hurt him. A lot. But it didn't kill him.

"You done? I kill you now?" Wicked said, with his cursed voice.

In that moment, Monica remembered the time we went out, just after Barney and Fairchild's honorable deaths.

"People die. It happens. Don't be a weakling now. That's not what your weak brother would've wanted for you" she said, to "comfort" me.

She was like that. Monica. She attacked and insulted the people she cared about the most, in order to strengthen them beyond belief. And it was exactly that what I needed to cheer me up and create the K-Team.

That's also why I love her.

I think she likes me. I think. We're friends, but I hope she, like me, wants something more.

Anyway, back to the present . . .

"The Deathbomb didn't kill him. How the hell's that possible?" Mark said. He wasn't afraid, probably because he was in Damaken, and it kinda kills your fears. Monica wasn't afraid either; she wasn't the type of girl to be scared.

"Okay, so this is what we do. One punch of his and we're done for. I'm going to sever his neck, but you'll have to cover me. Can you do that?" Monica asked Mark.

"There's no way you'll succeed." Mark replied, still in Damaken.

"Watch me." Monica replied cocky.

She attacked Wicked; he tried to hit her, but Mark's dark magic had diverted the path of Wicked's fist. Monica tried to punch Wicked, but she missed, resulting in her right hand being 2 centimeters away of Wicked's neck.

"You now die, little girl." he said, as he tried to backslap her.

"Hoopling: Total Terrorization!" Monica said, creating a kontetti field superfast, with about 1000 kontetti rays, and all were pointed at Wicked's neck. Counting the massive damage he had suffered from Mark's Dark Deathbomb, there's no way he'll survive this. I mean, laser precision kontetti rays after a blast capable of scarring the earth to an unbelievable extent?

The tyrant was brought down.

"We should go meet the others. Loser." Monica said, mocking Mark.

". . . Fine." Mark replied, ashamed, exiting Damaken.

CHAPTER 20

VENDETTA ACHIEVED

That leaves Bridgeman and I. We were chasing Revia, but there was no trace of him at the Clanhunters base. Guess he bailed out once he realized his minions had died.

"What now?" Matej asked.

"I don't know. Where is he?" I shouted, very loudly, at that. Why, you ask? Because I was three quarters finished with getting my vendetta for Barney. And I owe it to Fairchild to kill his murderer's deputy, after all, he did kill an Uncle. It just fills me with anger that we haven't found him yet.

"Don't shout." Matej said.

"We will find him. And kill him."

But we had to go back to St. Atlas to meet up with the others. Great. Another setback. We should've already finished.

"Is it done?" Mimmy asked.

"No." Matej responded, coldly.

"What do you mean NO? We succeeded, why didn't you?" Mimmy shouted, angrily.

"Their opponent was the toughest. The probably couldn't locate him, they weren't as lucky as us." Tommy said, having my back.

"So what are you going to do about it?" Sebastian asked.

"We're going to hunt him down and kill him." I replied.

"Woo! Time for fun!" Mimmy said, as she started stretching and hitting her knuckles one against the other.

"Matej and I. We are going to hunt him down and kill him." I said, making it clear to Mimmy that she or anyone else for that matter cannot go with us.

"I've dragged you all into this. The enemy is powerful." I continued, knowing fully well that that's not enough to convince them to back out.

"So what? We can take care of ourselves, you know . . ." Lucy objected.

"You know we're strong enough to kill him." Sebastian added.

"No"—Matej replied—"Martin and I are."

"This is no time to be cocky!" Monica shouted.

"We will beat him, but what if he kills one of you? The less, the better. Look, I don't know you all personally, but I do know you're all pretty strong. However, this is something Martin and I must do together." Matej spoke.

That seems to have done the trick. Everybody was quiet again.

"Be safe" Alice said, as the K-Team dispersed.

This was the last time I saw the K-Team with these members.

"Ready for this?" Matej asked.

"I was born ready." I replied.

"Let's go." he concluded our little chat.

We then went to look for Revia. The man gives the phrase "impossible to find" a whole 'nother meaning.

3 hours later, it seemed we got lucky. There was a guy, in the mountains, obsessed out of his mind. We came to him, somewhat by accident.

"What's wrong, random guy who we just met?" Matej said, already annoyed by the white-haired lunatic we just encountered. I looked at him, and he replied: "What? Get away!" as if he didn't realize that what he just said was completely crazy.

"Forever . . . ALIVE!" the guy shouted.

"What are you babbling about?" Matej quickly responded, not fascinated by the words coming out of the obsessed guy's mouth.

"It's . . . not human!" the guy screamed and ran away from us, as quickly as he could.

"Should we chase him?" I asked.

"No, he's a nut job." Matej responded with ease. He wasn't worried. Matej. That's good; 'cause that means I've got nothing to worry about. At least I think.

We crashed for the night in the village. Think it was the village of Dartngenn's people. They are very friendly people; as they let me and Matej crash there free of charge. They hold no special powers, just kindness. Though in Battleworld, kindness could easily be the rarest virtue.

"You fine gentlemen all good here?" the owner of the house we were staying in asked.

"It's okay." both Matej and I said at the same time. Although these people took us in kindly, we couldn't let our guard down. No warrior ever could.

We did ask him about the lunatic from earlier, but he gave us no reply. Just before I went to sleep, I overheard some people talking about some deity of theirs. They described it as: "The one that shall not leave us". I'm wondering what that is. Just like I wonder about that lunatic.

We woke up at 9 a. m. Time to continue the hunt.

"I'm tired again. Let's sleep." Matej said, complaining, like usual. You should have seen him during the Killhunt. He slept 90% of the time we spent locating Lady Insect's lair.

"No. Stop whining about everything." I told him. He was really starting to annoy me. I know he didn't have any interest in my vendetta, and is only here for support and as a friend, but that doesn't mean he gets to rest until this is over. We left the village, and walked for about 15 minutes.

"We're not getting anywhere, let's just go." he replied.

"I'm not so sure about that." I responded.

And there it was. Right in front of us, on the top of the highest mountain, a spooky, black castle. Nothing like the OSW castle; this castle was poorer and smaller. And way less decorated. Still, it was a castle.

"Think Revia's there?" Matej asked me.

"Worth checking out." I answered.

We went into the castle.

"Anyone here?" Matej shouted.

Like Revia was gonna answer. Then, I heard a movement. Behind me.

"Stodyanna: Plasma Bolt!" I shouted, performing a Plasma Bolt on him. It hit him head on. I activated it, and did a handspring backwards about 10 meters; Matej had already waited for me there, he ran behind when I activated the Plasma Bolt. It was Revia. How did I know? Just a second before my Plasma Bolt exploded, a few seconds after its activation, that is, I saw his face. Exactly how I imagined him. Mid-length, sliced-back white hair.

"Well, that was easy." Matej said.

"And that concludes my vendetta. Let's go." I added.

"Ok" Matej said, relieved, thinking he was going to get some more rest. He thought wrong.

"Thought you had already killed me?" Revia said, as he snuck up behind Bridgeman. He took out his sword and tried to stab him, but Matej slowed time and evaded.

"WHAT? Why is he still alive?" Matej shouted at me, shocked.

"I-I don't know!" I shouted as well, nervously, wondering how he had managed to survive my Plasma Bolt.

"I will kill you. You will not kill me." he said, full of confidence, smiling.

"Watch me." Matej replied.

"Bridgeman: Imperial Time Stop x 100!" he shouted, slowing time.

"Also this: Water Body Trap!" Matej continued. Water came out of nowhere, and it formed an armor-like trap around Revia's arms and legs.

"Oh no, I'm trapped." Revia said sarcastically.

"Water Dismember." Matej finished the attack.

Water had tightened up to the point of breaking Revia's arms and legs; the water was just too dense.

Then, as Revia's legs and arms were pulled away from the rest of his body by Matej's water, a purple force suddenly appeared. It stitched the limbs back to the body; not like my Anena: Regeneration, more like a puzzle solving itself.

Revia, regenerated, rushed to me with his sword (a slim, black, sharp blade), and tried to stab me. He succeeded. Right in the heart.

"One down" Revia said, laughing like a maniac.

I came behind him and had stabbed him in his heart with my Kelemen swords. I was in Damaken. A new feature I had gained from training under both my grandma and Sebastian in one day; I can now use the Kelemen swords while in Damaken.

"Kelemen Seal!" I shouted, ending Revia's life. Or so I thought. It was an illusion; the real Revia was 20 m away from me, laughing still. Matej, however, teleported behind him and stabbed him in the heart, with his ice. He had made an ice pick. Revia took it out of his heart and rushed to me, and I rushed to Matej. So now, Matej and I were on one side of the castle's main room, and Revia was on the other.

"Kelemen, I was wondering, how did you survive my sword?" Revia said, making his sword out to be something special, when in reality it wasn't.

"I used my Damaken: Dead Body Switch. Just before you "killed" me, I switched my body with another, half dead body I had collected." I answered, being a smartass and all.

"Wanna end this? All we have to do is trap him for eternity." Matej had figured out.

"Ok. Go!" I shouted, with utter enthusiasm.

"Stodyanna: Plasma Bolt!" I screamed. Yet another Plasma Bolt, my energy's running low.

"It won't do you any good." Reiva said, full of self-confidence, not dodging my attack.

It hit him.

"Matej Water Tsunami!" Matej shouted, from above. Yes, my Plasma Bolt was a diversion for Matej's grand attack. It trapped Revia in the ocean water. A giant ocean, fitting for a life-sentence.

"Now, all clan members can rest safely, without the danger of the Clanhunters." I proclaimed.

"See ya!" I heard Matej shout very loudly at Revia, mocking him.

Revia tried to say something, but to no avail. Doomed to spend his very long life in chains of water.

CHAPTER 21

OSW VS. BRIGHTLESS

First thing I saw in the morning on my way to the OSW castle was a black cat. I'm not superstitious, so I guess it doesn't mean something bad is going to happen, but it doesn't hurt to stay cautious.

"Hey everyone." I said.

"What's this?" I continued, looking at a paper that was on the desk.

"It's a list of some Brightless society members." Phil said.

"Plus the leader, Verbringer." added David.

Katarina nodded. I looked at the list, and saw their names. Nobody important or known to me, besides the Pentoline clan member, Svetlana.

"We'll do it this way:

Dariah, Anny, you go after the first two.

Phil, David, the next pair.

Katarina and Alice, you chase Svetlana and her partner.

Claire and Mary, attack the last two.

Martin and I will go for the leader and the deputy." Matej said, confidently.

Dariah Skyliner is a long blond-haired teenage girl, she is from the Skyliner clan; she can create time-space portals that can teleport you to any place in the skies; as opposed to Anny Groundliner's time-space portals that can teleport you to all places on the ground. Anny is her Anena; she, on the other hand, is a long red-haired, blue-eyed teenage girl.

"Fine. That's acceptable." David responded.

"I agree. And I believe everyone does. Right?" Katarina bossed us around. I wonder why, considering she's probably jealous as hell that Matej and I got Verbringer.

"Right." we all said.

"Go." David dismissed us.

In the first two hours, Anny and Dariah beat their opponents (just like Claire and Mary), and Phil and David had just met with theirs. And although Brightless's sergeant, Det, fought admirably, he could not stop the OSW leader, even with the help of his muscular bodyguard. Phil barely needed to fight.

Next were Alice and Katarina versus Svetlana and her boyfriend, Casa. They finished their battle quickly. Casa's mind games were no match for the Firod prodigy.

The important part of this battle was Svetlana. Katarina and Svetlana are both of the same clan (Pentoline), but Katarina is primarily a Ryunichi, so, with the help of her vampires, Katarina managed to destroy Svetlana. And I do mean destroy. Rip apart, mutilate, whatnot.

The Brightless were always a sworn enemy of the OSW. The OSW has no particular clothing style, but the Brightless, of course, just need to have white outfits. Both societies have great speed, but the OSW are the good guys, while the Brightless aim to kill anyone and everyone standing in the way of them completing their goal. And what might that goal be? That's a real mystery. They call it "The Revival". Simple as that.

But now, the only ones who remain of the infamous Brightless society are the last surviving Uncle, Uncle Verbringer, and his right hand man.

CHAPTER 22

PRODIGAL KIDS

I don't love anything like I love Friday morning. This Friday morning in particular. Why? Because, finally, and I do mean finally, the 8th graders managed to graduate. That means no more of them mocking us because we're younger. And everyone is happy about it. And everyone is practicing their attacks. Everyone, that is, except Monica and I. The two of us are talking. Falling in love with each other, smiling, flirting, discussing the difficulties of subjects taught at school . . . Doing just about everything.

"You know, we should be practicing our techniques." I told her.

"Yes, we probably should." she smiled. Her smile was the cutest one I ever saw in my entire life. It was the only thing I needed.

"Then why don't we?" I asked her, smiling back.

"Come on, let's celebrate the fact that yet another generation left St. Atlas." she said, grabbing my hand.

"But you never know what might happen; in what situation you might be put." I continued, annoying her. I just had a bad feeling because mine and Matej's hunt for Verbringer didn't bear fruit.

"The situation I am in right now is lame, because this one guy is really getting on my nerves. I would really like to, y'know, kill him." she started raging.

"Try it." I grinned.

"Was waiting for you to say that." she quickly responded.

"Hoopling: Monica Arena!" she shouted.

Ah. Hoopling and their arenas. A Hoopling's arena differs from one Hoopling to another. Their arena is a field of kontetti, arranged so that it looks like something that particular Hoopling imagines, so it's easier in the future (with their arena activated) for them to execute Hoopling attacks the way they want them, as opposed to doing them without the arena.

Her arena was a warehouse, empty and large. Extra large.

"Monica Arena Shutdown!" Monica said, as her arena sprung infinite guns; and fired kontetti lasers from those guns. In a situation like this, Matej usually slows time. But I need to get used to fighting strong opponents on my own. And in this situation, best I can come up with is Lady Insect's stem shield. I quickly got to Monica. I am a lot faster than her, after all.

"Stodyanna: Plasma Bolt!" I shouted.

"Enrik: Energy Flow Stop!" shouted Elaine, who was watching our battle. She stopped my energy, therefore my Plasma Bolt, because if she hadn't, I would have launched it at Monica. Of course, I would've stopped the attack before it harmed her, but Elaine just had to show off.

"You admit I'm better now?" I asked her, smiling, ignoring Elaine.

"Pure luck." she answered, hastily, deactivating her arena. I smiled.

"Wanna get out of this place?" she asked me.

Now, if this was a normal girl, I wouldn't budge and risk getting shouted at by my class-mistress for skipping school, but since this is Monica Hoopling, all I have to say is:

"Yeah, this is getting boring."

I kinda like the risk. She smiled as we went outside.

"Wait you can't-" Elaine said, without finishing her sentence as we ran away.

We were just walking, holding hands, and talking about our friends.

"So, who do you hang out with at school?" she asked me, interested in my friends. Guess she's in love with me about now. I hope she is.

"Elaine. Now that Barney's dead we're closer than ever." I answered her, plainly. I still have trouble saying his name. Not in front of Monica, though.

"How close exactly?" she asked, fixing her hair.

"Best friends close. Nothing more, nothing less." I answered Monica, to ease her of her jealousy.

"Anyone besides Elaine?" she asked.

"Matthew, Michael, Johhny, and Proshko." I replied.

"Oh." she said happily, because none of the above were girls.

"Does any of them even come close to you in power?" she asked, complimenting me.

"One."

"Who?"

"Proshko. He is far stronger than either Fairchild or I." I answered.

"Good one. Seriously, is there anyone you can spar with, besides me, of course?" she asked again, thinking what I said was a joke.

"No. I mean it. You haven't worked with Proshko closely, so you don't know this; but when he fights for something or someone, he's a whole different man. He has such power hidden in him, but it's like he can't release it." I answered.

"Seriously?" she asked me.

"I don't know. He is maybe just ordinary, but, around him, I just felt . . . weak. Since I got the Kelemen swords, that feeling's changed; now I feel equal to him.

But you're right, it's probably nothing. Most likely, because I've got no one as strong as myself, I make my best male friend at my school come close, when he's really not." I said, shrugging my shoulders.

"You know what?" she said.

"Wha-" I didn't finish my sentence, when she grabbed me and kissed me. It was my first kiss. I couldn't even move. The best thing about it? It was her first kiss, as well. Needless to say, it was amazing. Like 50 000 volts of my Stodyanna clan techniques coursing through my body every nanosecond. I simply felt love.

"I love you." I said when the kiss was over, standing there like an idiot.

"Lova ya too." she said, kissing me again.

So, I started caring about someone in a whole different way.

I never felt something like this with Elaine.

CHAPTER 23

A WARRIOR'S PRIDE

During the time Monica and I had been kissing each other, things at school stayed the same.

"Guys, do you feel something?" Elaine asked all the other people from our 7th C.

"Michael, check it." Jaden said, feeling a bit distressed.

Jaden J, a brown-haired brown-eyed thirteen-year old boy who uses his skateboard for attacks, is the leader of our class. His deputy, Tom, uses his giant snake and her toxins to beat his enemies.

Michael quickly adapted to a hunting dog in order to smell an intruder. But just as he started to smell something, a person came from nowhere and punched him, knocking him hard into a wall behind him, breaking both the wall, Michael's nose, and had it not been for Proshko's stiff earth platform that he used to ease Michael's fall, his spine.

Out of the smoke emerged a woman.

"Trueearth: Trap Sphere" Proshko said, raising his left hand, but before he could finish, Matthew interrupted him.

"She was fast enough to break Michael. Don't try to trap her; it won't work."

"Gah . . . How dare she do that to Mich-" before Proshko could finish, she ran to him, grabbed his right hand, and broke it in several places. She then proceeded to kick Proshko, knocking him into a wall.

"Such skill . . . Flawless in both precision and speed . . . she's powerful." Tom said.

"Thank for pointing out the obvious." said Elaine, as she rushed to the woman.

"I am not going to let some mysterious character come here and kill me or my friends like you killed Barney!" she shouted, getting closer to the woman, who wasn't moving.

"Barney Buttons? He died with that Fair Child, didn't he?" the woman spoke.

"H-How did you know that? Who are you? Are you one of them?" Elaine shouted.

"Calm down, Enrik." Heather said, trying to calm Elaine down. Heather is a girl in my class, very tall, blonde hair and blue eyes. Not as pretty as other blondes with blue eyes I've met, but pretty none the less.

"What do you want?" Heather continued, with a serious face.

The woman rushed to Heather and Victoria, who was standing next to Heather, and broke each of their right arms, and knocked them into a wall, the same wall she knocked Michael and Proshko into.

"Enrik: Heart Stop!" Elaine shouted.

The woman dodged the attack and then rushed to Elaine. Her Enrik shield protected her from the mystery woman's punches, causing damage to the her; however, the woman took the damage, broke the shield and hit Elaine in several places, broke her leg, and, you guessed it, knocked her into the same wall as the rest.

She repeated the process with . . . almost everyone from 7th C, apart from me of course, 'cause I was out with Monica. And apart from Barney, who was dead.

"Well whaddaya know, I actually had fun" the woman said.

6th B was observing this; but even Lucy couldn't stop this woman, so all they could do is watch and be afraid.

That was when Proshko rose.

"I-I won't let you hurt my friends!" he shouted.

"Proshko, this is no time to be a hero, get down!" Jaden J tried to grab him, but failed, because of his broken leg.

Proshko was often teased by almost everyone. He had very low self-confidence. He was the last guy you would see do this.

"N-No. I won't let this sadistic bitch ruin my life! Any of our lives!" Proshko shouted.

"Trueearth: Earth Fist!" he shouted, performing the Trueearth clan's strongest attack: The Earth Fist. He launched a giant fist of earth at her. For a while there, it seemed he was going to kill this woman.

"Heh. So I have to waste some energy, huh? Fine." she made a fist of kontetti and clashed it with Proshko's fist.

Normally, Proshko would win this clash. But considering that Proshko didn't have a lot of energy, and the woman was full, he was losing.

"Say bye-bye." she said, enjoying her supremacy.

Proshko remembered how his dad went down for killing his mother, a crime he did not commit, the weakening of the Trueearth clan, how both his brothers had perished saving their home in the war. He remembered his father's last words to him, clearly stating he is the Trueearth prodigy and that he, of all people, can show the world the true meaning of Trueearth.

The woman's attack closed in.

"I-I w-we will not end up the way Barney did . . . NEVER!" he said, as his earth fist prevailed over the woman's kontetti, which fired back at her, but she managed to dodge.

"So you're stronger than I thought?" the woman said.

"W-What?" she said, interested, looking at Proshko, after the smoke cleared up.

Proshko had changed. His earth armor manifested. It was different than before, it became like that of a knight. I later found out it was his skin, not his armor. He managed to harden his skin. He had reached a whole new transformation.

"Huh . . . so the myth is true, huh? You are the Trueearth prodigy. The one that comes every 5000 years . . ." she said. Proshko had no idea what she was talking about.

"Look, I don't know what you're saying; and I don't care." Proshko said angrily while he threw a massive pile of earth at the woman. She barely managed to dodge.

"So you wanna play, huh?" she provoked him.

Large rays of kontetti attacked both Proshko and the rest of the 7th C.

"Hector Shield!" Proshko said, as a giant wave-like shield appeared to protect them.

"Heh . . . well, this is it for you, prodigy . . ." the woman laughed.

Meanwhile, I had taken Monica to meet Matej. They began disliking each other the very second they met. And I liked that. Don't know why, though. Matej and I had to go hunting for Verbringer and his replacement, but first we were gonna go make sure Monica does her training with her class, not cut class. And I'm glad we did, or else we would have never made it in time.

"And why is this 'it' for me'?" Proshko asked, with a level of cockiness I never thought he had.

"Hoopling: Majestic!" the woman shouted, maniacally laughing.

A lot of kontetti fired, but Proshko managed to defend himself and 7th C with the Hector shield.

Then, suddenly, the kontetti lasers merged and created various animals. Butterflies, deer, and, after a while, every animal that represents peace and happiness. Some of the butterflies managed to get inside the Hector shield.

"N-No . . ." Proshko mumbled in fear.

"It's Majestic!" the woman shouted, sadistically grinning.

"Truearth: Total Defense!" Proshko screamed, defending his classmates with all the earth he managed to conjure up out of nothing, even the earth that was defending him. He was going to die. All the peaceful things and animals became dark; they shot kontetti rays at Proshko.

After the attack, the woman got back to her original position (before Proshko transformed).

"So now you're dead." she said, sadistically.

But he wasn't. When the smoke cleared, you could see clearly who took the fall for the Hoopling's strongest attack, Majestic.

It was Neron, my scorpion. And standing on his dead body you could clearly see Matej and I. We dropped Monica off with the the 6th graders (6th B).

"No . . . no way this is happening . . ." Monica said, with the most shocking expression I have ever seen her make in my entire life.

"Don't worry, M. Everyone's safe. Thanks to your boyfriend." Robert smiled, pointing at me.

"M-Matej that's" I said, but before I could finish he answered.

"Yes. By her robes, you can see that she is a Brightless."

She was the woman I saw in the graveyard that night.

"Who is she?" Matej said.

"That's not why I worry . . ." Monica replied to Robert.

"Then why?" he asked, raising his eyebrow.

"Annette! What is this?" Monica said, looking like she saw the devil himself.

"Why hello there sweetie." the woman replied.

Yes. That woman my brother had dated, and Verbringer's number 2, is Annette Hoopling.

"Damn it." Monica started crying.

"Monica, I know this is hard, but we have to beat her. If we don't . . ." Matej said.

"That's not why I said that." Monica responded.

"Then why is it?" Matej asked.

"It's because . . ." Monica started to answer, but I interrupted her.

"Annette is as strong as Voyager, if not stronger, right?"

". . . yeah." Monica answered, looking down.

None of us could hide the shock. Especially Matej.

His look, full of despair, pointed directly at Annette; and she realized it. In fact, she enjoyed it.

"Come on, I'm getting bored . . ." Annette said, grinning.

CHAPTER 24

WONDERKIDS

Let's take things back 11 years. Annette Hoopling is an 8th grader in St. Atlas.

"Classmaster, I've finished!" she said, full of enthusiasm.

That's what she was like. Always smiling, enjoying the better side of life. She had just finished her math test; the Hoopling were always good at math.

"Ah, excellent Annette, I wouldn't expect anything less from you." said her class-mistress, tech Tamzon, the kontetti tech. She was always proud of Annette, with her being the best and all.

"Um . . . class-mistress, may I . . ." she said, smiling innocently.

"Yes, Annette, you may." tech Tamzon replied, rolling her eyes.

"Thanks!" Annette replied gracefully.

Today was her and Voyager's 8th anniversary. They had been dating since kindergarten. Cute. Anyway, she came to their rendezvous point, a place near the children's playground, to find him waiting there with flowers.

"Aw! Are those for me? How cute!" she said as she kissed him.

"I also got you this." He said, giving her a golden flower.

"This flower will rot only when all things are set straight. It's rather a magical kind." he said as he put the golden flower around her neck. It circled her neck like a choker.

"Thanks! I love it! Of course, I got you something better." she responded.

"And what might that be?" he asked.

"It's a shirt! A cute one, at that. To get you to stop wearing all your suits, businessman." Annette said, smiling.

"Thanks, it's beautiful. Just like you." he said as he kissed her.

"Tomorrow we should select the high school we'd like to go to. The second step is getting accepted, but that's no problem for us." Annete said smiling.

Voyager put on a worried face.

"We ARE going to the Kontetti school, aren't we?" she asked, seriously.

"Yes, I know how much that means to you." he answered, relieved.

"And I love you, forever." he added. They hugged.

Two years passed. They were both now ending their second year. And it was their 10th anniversary. They were currently in front of the Kelemen house.

"We've been together whole morning. We should go to school." Voyager said.

"I can't. I'm sick." Annette said, with sadness.

"I know sweetie. Don't worry. The next time you see me, we are going to celebrate today's occasion." he said, smiling, holding her head, looking her in the eyes.

"Okay." she said, smiling at him, also looking him in the eyes.

"Take care!" he said, leaving.

"You too." she mumbled.

And that's the last time Annette saw Voyager.

12 hours later, she receives the information that he is dead.

She is shocked, terrified, petrified; she cannot move from all that awe, tears start raining down her face, her heart starts throbbing; only making it even harder to survive. She becomes truly dead inside.

8 years later, she starts engaging in the Brightless society. And here we are.

Once, when Uncle Verbringer recruited her, he tried to seduce her. She quickly broke his arm. He healed; but he never touched her again. That's what a Hoopling prodigy will do to you.

And THAT'S who Annette Hoopling is.

Chapter 25

Ruined Life

"Come on, who's first? The Clock or Voyager Jr.?" Annette said, smiling sadistically, like always.

"Or both at once? You know I'm always up for a little group fun . . ." she continued, mocking us.

"Why are you doing this?" I asked, still shocked. I didn't know Annette Vylona Hoopling at all. But I feel like I've known her my entire life.

"Not much of a reason, I'm just cleaning up the world of the OSW trash" she answered, meaning it.

Monica still looked at her sister, not believing her eyes.

"Let's begin." Annette started.

"Hoopling: Annette Arena" she shouted.

"Bridgeman: Imperial time stop x100!" Matej responded, slowing time.

"Stodyanna: Plasma Bolt!" I shouted, as I charged up lightning in my hand; it coursed throughout my whole body, and finally gathered in my hand.

Annette's kontetti hit us, but they were only strong as regular kontetti; due to Matej slowing time, therefore decreasing their speed, and ultimately, decreasing the number of shots fired in a split second.

I attacked her with my Plasma Bolt, but she managed to hit me right in my veins with her kontetti; and that stopped my attack. Plasma Bolt attack's one weak point.

She's the most precise person I had ever met.

She then broke Matej's arms, stopped a water attack he was preparing, and knocked him to the wall opposite of the one where my entire class was. She tried to break my arms; luckily, because my Kelemen swords were in them, she couldn't.

But she did break my legs, and knocked me into the aforementioned wall.

Matej used the Bridgeman clan's ancient leaves passed down from generation to generation to heal his broken arms, and I used my Anena regeneration to heal my broken legs.

We were both very much exhausted from this.

"Wanna go all Beachfighter on her ass?" Matej asked me, smiling. What a sadist.

"Hell yeah." I quickly answered, immaturely smiling.

It was now time for and mine and Matej's combination warrior, but instead of the blue kontetti field and all that, we just have to combine our Anena seals.

"Come on, do it." Annette said, knowing full well what we're up to.

We then combined. It was one massive explosion of energy, at first.

Out of it came a dark red-brown-haired brown-eyed fourteen year-old. He was a lot hotter than Matej and I combined.

Killbridge. That's who we are now. He was nicknamed Beachfighter. Don't really know why, but it's cool.

"Now we get to see who's stronger." Killbridge said.

"Fine by me." she answered.

They exchanged a few blows, and were equally match, she was maybe a tiny bit stronger.

"Calling: Deathanchor!" she said, calling an anchor into battle. She held it with her hand, smiling.

"Is that . . . the Deathanchor?" Killbridge asked, with a partially shocked look on his face. Of course it was. And of course she just got a helluva lot stronger.

"Yes." Annette answered simply, seriously.

Let me explain. The Deathanchor was made a long time ago by a wizard. It's a simple weapon, actually, with two special features: a) It kills whoever it fatally wounds (including vampires, and combination warriors like Killbridge) b) It can become unstoppable and undodgeable with a human sacrifice.

So, anyway, she launched it at Killbridge. He dodged, and went for her. She dodged his fist, and countered with a kontetti attack. Killbridge slowed time, negated the attack, hit her with his legs, though she dodged and punched him, he evaded. That's when the anchor returned, like a boomerang. Killbridge dodged it again, but he took her next Hoopling attack head on. He was hurt, but he stayed as Killbridge and returned to our original position. She laughed.

"Ahahahaha. You're pathetic. Time to bring this to an end." she said.

"I couldn't agree more." Killbridge said.

"Attack of the Wicked" he added.

Ah, you could say that it's a new attack, named after that Clanhunter psychopath. Killbridge made a giant water wave and then electrocuted it. Yes.

Since either of us was born, Bridgeman and I could not feel the stress on the body because of water and lightning mixing. That's why we can work so well together.

Matej has a water bone, while I have a lightning bone.

A lightning bone helps one feel little if not (like me) none at all side effects from creating too much lightning, while a water bone does the same thing with water. Killbridge has both.

That wave we made started to make out Wicked's face. I guess we configured it that way because it's scary. Then we launched it at Annette, and she couldn't dodge it.

"Oh well." she said.

"And that's Killbridge for you."

I honestly thought it was done.

"Don't celebrate just yet." Monica said.

She didn't care about her sister, nor about us. She knew her sister was a criminal who didn't deserve to live and that I was doing the right thing, but she just couldn't cope with her sister dying, so she shut all her emotions down. She was like that.

"My sweet baby sister is right." Annette said.

"You're no longer my sister. You're just a pathetic excuse for a Hoopling." Monica said.

"Aw, how cute. Come here!" Annette screamed, as she quickly (much quicker than Killbridge could stop it; and much faster than her regular speed) grabbed Monica, and then returned to her original position.

"Y-You evil bitch! How dare you threaten me with your sister's life?" Killbridge said, very upset.

"That's Voyager Jr. in you talking, isn't it?

Well, I'm not here to hold her hostage." Annette said.

"Let me g-go!" Monica screamed as she felt her body being pierced.

"NO!!!" Killbridge shouted.

Annette had stabbed Monica with the Deathanchor.

"You monster!" he couldn't belive his eyes.

She paid no attention at all, she just launched her Deathanchor at him. It hit him, and knocked him into a wall behind him. It seems she has a fetish for knocking people into walls.

"Y-You trash! So that's why you took your sister . . ." we started.

". . . so that I can use her as a sacrifice to multiply the speed and precision of my Deathanchor. As a result, even your speed combined with Bridgeman Time Stop x whatever failed to help you dodge my deadly weapon" Annette continued.

"Deathanchor: Seal!" she shouted.

"N-No!" we shouted. We closed our eyes, embracing the end. But then . . .

The attack ended. And we were alive. We opened our eyes; only to see Monica's neck veins cut, damped in blood, and her facedown on the floor. Her blood just kept flowing out.

Monica had taken a pocket knife and she had cut her neck veins.

"She killed herself . . . in order to save us . . . she killed herself . . . in order to save us . . ." our united mind kept thinking. We removed the Deathanchor and threw it away.

"Y-You bitch! I'll kill you!" Killbridge shouted, as he charged at Annette.

"My sister . . . is dead." she said, looking like she saw the devil.

He charged at her, she used kontetti on her fist, to strengthen it, and charged at him, full force.

As a result, Killbridge was knocked into the Wall (yes, that's what I'm calling it now) and he split into Martin and Matej again.

I cried and I was very angry. Matej just looked . . . serious.

"You're dead! You cannot kill me! Hoopling-" Annette said, trying to perform a Hoopling attack.

Matej extended his arm in the form of ice, while I extended my arm in a form of lightning. Matej got in front of her, put his arm beneath her head, and kept a serious face. I got behind her, put my arm above her head, and tried to keep a serious face, while crying.

Then we sliced her head off.

Her head, full of blood, fell on the floor and her body bled out.

I went to Monica to check her pulse.

"Unbelievable! It's a miracle!" I said.

"Martin, I hate to break this to you, but she's dead." Matej said.

"Not yet. In a few minutes maybe. But not yet." I said.

"Let's go then, quickly." Matej said, with no emotion whatsoever. Maybe a bit of happiness and hope.

Mary Angel Helig was the last of the Helig clan; the healer clan. They all died from a disease, except for a few kids at the time, including Mary. She is the clan's prodigy; she can heal anyone who's not dead, except if it's from the fact that you wasted too much energy and you have none left.

We took Monica to Mary, who healed her.

"She's gonna have to remain here for a certain amount of time." Mary said.

When Mary heals an OSW, they're healed right away, because of the magic in their Anena seal, but when a person isn't OSW and does not have the Anena seal, it takes time to heal.

"Stay here, in the castle." she told Monica who had just regained consciousness.

"Monica, listen . . ." I started.

"Somehow, someday . . . I'll make all this right."

She cried.

"Martin, we really should . . ." Matej said, putting his hand on my shoulder.

"Yes. We should go. Bye." I said, as me Matej and I went to search for the man himself, Uncle Verbringer.

"Somehow, someday . . . I'll make all this right."

I wish I could believe that. I really do.

Chapter 26

The last survivor

Matej and I went to the Brightless HQ. It was a giant, white mirror house. Felt very religious to me. That's where Verbringer was. At this time, the others were long finished with their assignments. Now to complete the Killhunt, Matej and I are here to kill the good Uncle.

"Verbringer, where are you?" Matej shouted, as if he was going to answer.

"He won't answer, even if he's here . . ." I said, pointing out the obvious.

"I'm here, pretty boy." Verbringer said, appearing out of the blue. Oh you've gotta be fucking kidding me. I can't believe how retarded we all are. If any resident of Battleworld is actually reading this, please, DO NOT, under any circumstances, join the OSW. Never. Or you'll be with all the weird freaks.

Like I am, right now. And oh look, Verbringer just bursted out his slime.

You see Verbringer, for attacks, uses his slime, which he takes out of his mouth/vomits. Gross.

Anyway, it's big, and white. And it is actually a living organism, which Verbringer controls. Along with the Uncle power, the power that each Uncle has (it gives him additional energy), he is worthy of being the Brightless's leader.

"Bridgeman time stop x100!" Matej shouted.

He slowed time; so Verbringer's slime didn't hit him. Verbringer attacked him with Uncle energy; which Matej neutralized with his water. Verbringer rushed to Matej and knocked him 10 meters away.

I pulled a Plasma Bolt on him, which he dodged and countered with his slime; his slime then wrapped itself around my arm.

"Slime Bonebreak!" Verbringer shouted as his slime infiltrated in my muscles and completely broke my arm.

"That's the thing with Annette. Due to my slime, I'm even more precise than her." Verbringer said, grinning like an idiot.

He then blasted me with his Uncle power a few times. I was lying on the floor, barely alive. I slowly moved a finger in an effort to get up, so Verbringer saw that I was alive.

"Time to kill you! You're both Kelemen and OSW. I will enjoy killing you. This is for my clan!" Verbringer shouted, preparing an Uncle energy attack he wished to fire at me.

I didn't want to die; I was Voyager's legacy.

Matej Bridgeman was like me, in that aspect. When he was 5 (like I was when Voyager died), the Bridgeman raid happened. 5 Bridgemen, including Matej, were out camping in a deserted village.

That gave The Raiders (a group of 5 members, led by Katli Zynnick and his deputy, Kayen Vlayer, both rogues and escapees from their clan) a perfect opportunity to strike. The other two members were the Gandarra brothers, Khatem and Dalthum, feared as "The Strongest

Tag Team Ever". The crew was completed with Heath Interr, a brutal sword master. None of them remain alive today.

As they broke in the deserted village, they feasted their eyes on two women and two young boys.

"Christine! Take Matej and Marco and run!" said Ciara Bridgeman, Matej's mother. Marco was Matej's at that time three years old brother. Christine, Ciara's sister took them; but Matej screamed: "Mommy" and ran to his mum.

"Matej, run" his mom screamed. She then vomited blood.

Kayen Vlayer's one Vlayer sword killed Ciara before Matej's eyes. Matej rose up, and made a certain face. His face was full of anger, he was shaking; he was dreadfully aware of his impending pain, and had focused it all into his fists.

Heath emerged, with his giant sword, to kill Matej.

"And I come for the prodigy!" Heath shouted.

Of course, that's just what stupid Heath thought. The real Bridgeman prodigy was in the Bridgecastle.

As Heath's sword closed in on Matej, he dodged it, and with his tiny body, pumped a hole in Heath's large body. As Matej's whole body went through Heath, he ripped multiple organs, and in the end even killed him.

"You bastard!" the Gandarra brothers shouted at the same time.

Matej jumped, and so did Khatem and Dalthum. They turned their arms into mini-guns (the Gandarra clan specializes in turning parts of their body into weapons) and started shooting at him. He raised two pillars of water, which were dense, and protected himself from Gandarra's bullets. He then redirected the water towards them, rotting their arms, and decapitating them. He then returned to the ground, rushed to Vlayer and killed him quickly, with the water beneath Vlayer that had turned to ice beforehand, and Matej stabbing the now trapped Kayen Vlayer in the heart with an ice pick, resulting in his heart stopping and Matej killing him.

"Zynnick: Fire Overdose" Katli shouted, releasing a tremendous amount of fire and launching it at Matej, but to no avail. His water neutralized Katli's fire. Matej then took an ice blade and cut Katli's neck. And The Raiders were no more . . .

Why am I telling you this story?

Because now, when Verbringer is trying to kill me, Matej is running to my rescue. He stopped Verbringer's attack, and he had THAT look on his face. Again. For the second time in his life.

"Oh, you mad? Sorry for beating up your girlfriend." Verbringer said.

Matej wasted no time; he rushed to Verbringer, faster than Verbringer could get away, and punched him in the stomach, then knocked him in the air. He followed Verbringer into the air, hitting him on his way up. Verbringer spat out his slime, but Matej dodged it. The slime turned into Verbringer; while Verbringer (the one Matej was hitting up in the air) transformed into a slime. A reverse-substitution. Clever. The original Verbringer fell on the floor, and the slime had wrapped itself around Matej's arms, preparing to break them. Matej kept his face. You could see a single tear emerging from his eye. He then froze Verbringer's slime, knocked it, frozen, into the ground (destroying it in the process) and turned around so that he can crash back into the ground, land on Verbringer and kill him. Verbringer tried to run. He couldn't; Matej's water pipes had trapped him.

"Heh . . . Strongest Parasite Attack!" Verbringer shouted, as, out of his mouth, appeared a giant blob of slime, ready to hit Matej, who was still in the air. Matej had also made sure of that as well. He froze Verbringer's mouth; so he couldn't fire slime out of it. He also fortified his prison, so the ones Verbringer managed to shoot couldn't move, and would soon disappear. Matej was falling, trying to crash into the trapped Verbringer.

"Teardrop!" he shouted, as he called up all his Bridgeman Imperial Time Stop energy, all his water energy, and, most of all, all of his ice energy. As he was freefalling onto Verbringer, tears fell down his cheeks. Those tears froze, as did everything around him, except his fist, which was of purple color. He crashed into Verbringer, and hit him with his powered fist, full power.

"No!" Verbringer shouted, in pain.

Out of the ground emerged ice picks. A lot of them. They pierced through and killed Uncle Verbringer.

Matej felt peaceful, like he had avenged someone. And he did. He thought he was saving me, but while doing that, he was saving the world, saving the OSW, avenging my brother, and eliminating the whole Uncle clan.

I smiled. Because finally, finally, finally, I felt that justice for my brother had been achieved.

And it was thanks to my brother-in-arms, Matej Bridgeman.

CHAPTER 27

THE QUEEN

After I healed with my Anena regeneration, other members of the OSW came. All of them. We were all in our prime; except for Matej and I, we were exhausted as hell.

"So that's it, huh? You finally killed all the baddies my sister used to hang out with?" Monica said.

"You brought her?" I asked Mary.

"I . . . had to! We weren't gonna leave her alone in the castle!" Mary shouted at me.

She had a point. If we left Monica alone, and if someone were, to say, attack us, they would find Monica, still not fully recovered. Luckily, that won't happen.

"Yes, Monica, I believe we're all done." Matej said.

Bam. A sound. A very loud one, at that. Something just came out of the ground. We went outside the Brighthouse. Yes, that's what they call the Brightless HQ.

And then we saw her. A girl. A woman. Beautiful. Long red hair, grey eyes, all in white, a white dress with a giant, dark white cross as her symbol.

"W-We thought"—Phil started that—"Brightless's "The Revival" meant that they were going to revive members . . . not to set off a time bomb . . . which triggered when Verbringer died. I think so, at least. I can't see another reason." Phil said.

Mary grabbed Monica and hid her inside the Brighthouse. She then returned to us.

"Who are you?" Katarina asked aggressively.

"I am Queen XVI. of the Bright Dark." said this "Queen".

Great. While we have no official leader, the Brightless get their own freakin' queen.

Well, we're done for.

For about 5 minutes everyone was trying something;

Katarina was trying to trap Queen with her hair,

Phil was wasting all his energy on his kontetti attacks,

David was basically shifting ground with his earth techniques,

Matej, with a low level of energy, was making a freakin' tsunami,

Alice called Tannimi, and did the Tannimi bomb,

Dariah and Anny were trying to trap her using teleportation, and all that while I rested. Huh.

"I'm sick of this bitch!" Katarina shouted.

"Ryunichi: All my exes!" she continued angrily, as she called about 1000 vampire brainwashed guys.

All the attacks above, including the 1000 exes, failed to even damage The Queen. She made a barrier in front of her which no one could get through.

"Anny! Let's combine. Martin, Matej you form Killbridge. Now!" Dariah shouted. Oh it's on. It's time for The Queen to meet the best guy ever. Daranny was quickly formed out of Dariah and Anny, and Killbridge stepped on the scene fast enough. Faster than you could say "You're dead".

"OSW Anena: Calling Mr. Perfect!" Killbridge and Daranny shouted. This was the strongest attack of the OSW, they (Killbridge and Daranny) called a magical human-like being that couldn't be beaten by anyone; henceforth the name, Mr. Perfect.

> "I am your bright beginning and your end that's
>   full of holes
> I am your light that shines bright and the dark
>   that eats away your souls
> I am your earth, I am your sky
> I am your reality, I am your lullaby
> I am not the one who will save you, I am not such
> I will salvage you from this pathetic life, I can
>   guarantee you that much." he said.

He was a blond-haired, black-eyed guy that teenage guys would describe as "perfect", because he is the strongest. And teenage girls would describe him as "perfect" because he is hot as hell.

> "You say you are my beginning and my end;
> But do you mean that, or do you pretend?
> You say that light is bright, yes,
> But what about those of us who are brightless?
> You say you won't save me, supposing you could
> But even if you could, why you should?" The Queen
>   replied, also poetically.

So now we're officially in the dead poet land.

Three seconds later, Perfect's dead, and The Queen is unharmed. The Queen has a shield; and it shields her from EVERYTHING. And I do mean EVERYTHING.

It's a white aura-like thing in front of her.

After Perfect died, Killbridge and Daranny quickly separated into Matej, Anny, Dariah and me.

"This is it for us, guys." Katarina said, and for the first time in her life, at least since I've known her, admitting defeat.

"Dariah, Anny, form Daranny again. I'm going to kill the bitch myself." I said. There we go.

"And I've got just enough energy to do it." I continued.

"But you have no energy." Matej said, worried.

"Exactly." I replied, and jumped 30 meters up. Yeah, I can do that. Almost everyone here can. Once you reach a certain level of speed, you can jump farther up than regular people.

There are four lightning clans, from weakest to strongest: Padyanna, Quanna, Radyanna, Stodyanna.

And I'm about to show her the strongest attack of the strongest of the four.

"Get ready for this, Queen!"

"Stodyanna: Divine Plasma Bolt!" I shouted, as in my hand appeared tremendous, massive, gigantic amounts of lightning. Strong enough to scar the earth itself.

"Ha-Ha! My shield will defend me!" The Queen shouted.

"What's Martin doing pulling off an attack like that? With his current energy level, he'll . . ." Matej said, fearfully, being afraid to finish that sentence.

"Die." Daranny said. She was formed. Good.

As I was closing in on The Queen, she heightened up her defenses. Which is right where I wanted them: in front of her.

"SkyGroundliner: Time-space hole!" Daranny shouted.

A hole, like one Killvla likes to make, formed in front of The Queen, she could see it clearly. And then, one formed behind her; one which she could not see.

Me and my lightning fell into the hole, and came out the other hole.

"N-No?!" The Queen said, trying to move her defenses from front to back. She succeeded, but I managed to slightly damage her, and then we both fell.

I got inside of her defense shield, with my hand shoved in her ribs.

"Matej . . . You have to do it." Daranny said.

Matej cried. A lot. Everyone watched, with sorrow.

"Die!" I shouted.

"And how exactly am I going to die?" she asked me, with an egoistical smirk.

"Matej, now!!!" Daranny shouted impatiently.

Matej continued to cry.

"Kaboom." I said, as my lightning exploded; the explosion's range being 500 meters in all directions. Luckily we were in an abandoned area. Shame about the Brighthouse, though. Great architecture.

"Gah . . . Bridgeman: Imperial Time Stop x 20 000!!!" Matej screamed, crying beyond belief. Time slowed a lot. So much, that, in fact, you could see little rocks being fried to oblivion by my lightning, along with me and The Queen. Everyone from the OSW escaped, though Matej hesitated: he wanted to die with me. But he didn't, because he knew that isn't what I wanted for him.

And he was right.

Everything became nothing. Not that there was much of anything to begin with.

All the OSW members rushed to my dead body.

Mary tried to heal me; knowing full well she couldn't.

David patted Matej on the shoulder and didn't mouth a single word. David Trueearth left speechless? Unheard of.

Monica ran away from the Brightless HQ back when Killbridge formed. She took that as her cue for "run".

Good thing she did.

And then, a bright, white light started to shine out of my body.

Everyone looked in marvel; no one could hide their shock. They saw Mary, not as a human, but as an angel.

"What is this?" Claire asked.

"It's my true form. I am the long lost Lifegod." Mary said, revealing her true identity.

We all of course knew who Lifegod was, the god of life, one that can breathe life, opposed to the Deathgod, the one that takes life away. Though no one, even Claire, her Anena, knew Mary was her.

I don't remember much, besides the white light ushering me through the darkness that was death.

And after giving life, the Lifegod was supposed to die, but she didn't. She went in my Kelemen swords. And she would remain there, as a part of me, forever.

"Welcome back, slick" were the first words I had heard after my rebirth. They were, of course, from Matej Bridgeman, my Anena.

We all went to celebrate, and then returned to our schools. All this hunting finished right before another school day started, of course.

I saw Monica. She was different; she didn't want to talk to me, and she ran and cut class. I guess it's normal, considering the circumstances.

"Eh, it's all right." I told Elaine.

"What do you mean "All right?" I was worried because of you all day!!!" she shouted, slapping me.

"By the way, Monica Hoopling? Even YOU can do much better . . ." she said, obviously disrespecting me.

"Huh, and since when are YOU the judge?" I replied.

I then ran to Proshko.

"Hey, badger! I mean, my Lord. Forgot I was talking to the Trueearth prodigy, otherwise I would have been on my best behavior." I said, smiling.

He smiled back.

"You're not so bad yourself, Killman." he replied, still smiling.

That's when I went to Neven.

"School is 'bout to end. Just a few more days . . . and bam—summer. How did you like this year?" I asked him.

"It was great"—he replied—"but not nearly as great as the next one is going to be."

If Martin and his friends want to survive their 8th grade and save everyone, they will have to know all the secrets, they will have to beat all the odds, and ultimately, they will have to find

The Kids That Led To Peace